THE FREAK

THE FREAK

Book One of The Freak Series

Carol Matas

KEY PORTER BOOKS

Library and Archives Canada Cataloguing in Publication

Matas, Carol, 1949–
The freak / Carol Matas.

Originally published: 1997.

ISBN-13: 978-1-55263-930-6, ISBN-10: 1-55263-930-4

I. Title.

PS8576.A7994F74 2007   jC813'.54   C2007-903926-X

The publisher gratefully acknowledges the support of the Canada Council for the Arts and the Ontario Arts Council for its publishing program. We acknowledge the support of the Government of Ontario through the Ontario Media Development Corporation's Ontario Book Initiative.

We acknowledge the financial support of the Government of Canada through the Book Publishing Industry Development Program (BPIDP) for our publishing activities.

Key Porter Books Limited
Six Adelaide Street East, Tenth Floor
Toronto, Ontario
Canada M5C 1H6

www.keyporter.com

Text design and formatting: Marijke Friesen

Printed and bound in Canada

07 08 09 10 11 5 4 3 2 1

For my pals Susan Bowden, Margaret Buffie,
Jacqui Good, and Maureen Hunter.
We keep each other laughing.

ONE

THERE IS A SAYING, IT GOES SOMETHING LIKE, "Life is what happens while you're making other plans." I can relate to that in a major way.

My life was orderly, neat, and pretty happy. I had just turned fifteen and had spent the summer at our cottage at Falcon Lake—my last non-working summer so I took full advantage. Lots of sun, sleeping in, swimming. My younger brother, Martin, was there, and so was his friend Jamie and my best friend, Susie. My dad stayed out with us all summer. He teaches math at the downtown university and he could work at the cottage. Mom came out for two weeks at the end of July, otherwise she drove out for weekends—she is a psychologist and needed to see her patients during the week.

I had everything planned. I was going to finish high school with super high marks and then take my pick of all the math scholarships being offered—I'm something of a whiz in both math and science. I knew that there was a logical reason for everything and that if one just stayed focused life could be controlled.

Hah!

I didn't know anything.

A week into August we all went to Wednesday bingo at the Falcon Lake town site—that's the biggest social event of the week out there. Of course at home we wouldn't be caught dead going to bingo (me and my friends), but it's considered sort of cool and retro out at the lake. A few days later Dad was driving me into the city 'cause I'd spiked a fever, a high fever, and my neck was so stiff I couldn't move it. He figured I'd caught some kind of bug at the bingo game—all those people crowded together like that. I was in a bad way by the time we got to the city so he took me right to the children's hospital.

By the time we got there I was delirious. I was admitted right away I guess—diagnosis: meningitis. And I don't know when exactly, but I almost died. And that's when everything changed.

~

The Freak

I am looking down at myself from the ceiling. Nurses are running into my room, my mom is screaming at them to help me. I want to tell her I'm fine, I feel great, and then I see myself, lying on the hospital bed, all pale, not breathing. A doctor runs into the room, then another one, they're doing stuff, but suddenly I'm in this long dark tunnel and I see a light at the other end, it's so bright, I have to get there and I travel really fast, I'm thinking maybe I'm travelling at the speed of light and suddenly I'm *in* this light—it's incredible. I can't even explain how it feels. It's like all the love in the entire universe is right there with me, it's, it's *unimaginable*. And then a tall figure stands before me and beside it, because I can't tell if it's a man or a woman, is my Zaida, my grandfather who died just last year. He smiles at me.

"Zaida!" I exclaim.

He takes my hand. "How's my little jewel?" he says. Just the way he used to. I'm so happy to see him.

"It's not your time yet," says the other presence. "You'll have to go back."

And then, I'm back in my bed in the hospital, and Mom is crying, Dad is crying, Marty is crying, and I smile at them and say, "I just saw Zaida," and then they look all shocked and they start to cry even harder. I let them cry and I go to sleep. I'm really tired.

I wake up on and off. I don't feel delirious or weird any more, just like someone knocked me on the head with a hammer, then put all my bones and muscles through some kind of a grinder. But I start to get better fast.

My room is full of flowers and teddy bears and cards. The nurses are pretty nice, when they have time to check on me. Mom grumbles constantly about cutbacks to health care and how there aren't enough nurses and soon we'll all be lying on the floor like in some Third World country. It *is* pretty bad. A couple of times my IV goes dry because the nurses are too busy somewhere else to come and change it.

Anyway, they finally take out the IV and they try to feed me this sick hospital food—meat with gravy. What happened to tea and toast? Mom rounds up some toast for me and Dad brings me Snapple iced tea from the cafeteria.

I have a roommate, of course. There's no such thing as a private room any more, apparently. But whenever the roommate's older brother comes to visit, something really weird happens. I keep seeing him limping and yet, when I look closer, he's not limping. I think that fever did something to my brain.

Finally, they say I can go home. I'm all packed up, and my roommate's older brother limps in, his leg in a cast. He smiles at me sheepishly. "I broke it falling down the stairs, do you believe that?"

I say something appropriate and then my mom calls me, "Come on, Jade. Dad's brought the car around. Let's go home."

And I realize that Mom is sort of covered in this really bright happy light, and I blink my eyes but it won't go away.

Well, I think, I *did* have a really high fever. It's probably the result of that. It's—and then suddenly, I remember what happened to me. I stop.

"Mom," I say, clutching her arm, "did I, like—almost die or something?"

She goes pale and says, her voice shaking, "Your heart stopped and you stopped breathing. But they brought you back."

"I saw Zaida," I say, "and an angel."

"Really?" She pauses. "Well . . . I've done a fair amount of reading about this and it's quite common. It's called a near-death experience. Just the brain reacting in a positive way to get you through the trauma."

That's logical, I guess. "But it was so real," I say.

"Of course it was, honey. When you're inside a dream it feels real, too, doesn't it?"

"I guess."

"Come on, Dad's waiting."

Of course, there's always a logical explanation. The kid with the cast waves goodbye. A shudder runs down my spine.

TWO

I FEEL TIRED ONCE I'M HOME AND FALL ASLEEP as soon as I get into my own bed. My room feels like heaven to me—so quiet, so clean. I'd painted it a deep forest green at the beginning of the summer and now I cuddle under my comforter and fall asleep in seconds. When I wake up it's not because a nurse needs to take my blood pressure or my neighbour is moaning, it's just because I've slept long enough.

Of course, Baba has brought over chicken soup, and she sits with me while I eat it. Baba is seventy-two. She does aerobics every day. She misses Zaida a lot but has a very busy life with her friends and her volunteer work. She loves politics and there's always a campaign to work on.

"You gave us quite a scare," she says.

"I dreamed I saw Zaida," I tell her, "when I almost died."

"Was it a dream?" Baba asks.

I hesitate. Mom says it was, but I have *never* felt anything so real.

"I guess so," I reply.

"I talk to him all the time," she says, very matter-of-fact.

I laugh. "You mean you imagine what he'd say to you if he were here, right?"

"No," she says firmly, "I talk to him. He told me he'd seen you. And that you'd been sent back."

"But, but, how did you know that?"

"I already said," she repeats, "he *told* me."

I guess my jaw must be hanging open or something because she smiles. "Don't look so shocked, sweetie," Baba says. "Don't you believe in an afterlife?"

"No!" I say. "Of course not. There's no afterlife because there's no God. What kind of God would make such a horrible, cruel world? It's up to us to put it all in order."

"I didn't say it wasn't up to us to make the world better," Baba says, "although order is something else altogether. But that doesn't mean that there isn't a God."

My head starts to hurt.

"Oh, I'm sorry, darling. I can see this is too much for you. You've had your soup, now you go back to sleep."

I nod, and then curl up under the covers.

"Baba," I mutter, "don't drop the bowl."

There's a crash, and I look up to see the bowl in a million pieces.

"What did you say, dear?"

"Nothing," I reply, thinking I must have startled her into dropping it. Still, what on earth had made me think of that in the first place? I guess she must have been holding it funny.

When I wake up I feel well enough to go downstairs to watch TV. There's some show on about these people who love their pets better than their spouses.

"He loves that snake more than me," complains a blond with dyed hair and more make-up than a circus clown. "No wonder," I say aloud to her, "the snake's better looking than you are!"

"Oh, you must be feeling better," Mom says, coming into the room. "You're talking to the TV again."

Okay, I admit it. I talk to the TV all the time. Why not?

"What's wrong?" I say to Mom.

"Oh, nothing," she answers, "just Marty. I *told* him to call if he wasn't going to be here for dinner . . ." She stops. "How did you know anything was wrong?"

I shrug. "I don't know. You must've looked mad."

"Well, you're definitely better. Reading my mind again and everything."

I've always been able to "read" the minds of everyone in our family. Mom says I have a very acute awareness of body language and how the tone of voice changes if someone is upset. We call it mind reading, but only as a joke.

"If I were you I'd make Marty come home for dinner," I say to Mom.

"Why? Want him here your first night home?"

"No. I just think he shouldn't eat at Doug's."

"Did I say he was eating at Doug's?"

"Yeah, you must've."

"Oh, I'll let him be," Mom says. "Only a week left until school. He needs his freedom."

Mom isn't a psychologist for nothing. She has a theory about everything.

I eat more soup then go back to bed. As I'm dozing in my room listening to the Jaw Breakers I hear a big ruckus. Marty is moaning and groaning and soon I hear him throwing up in the bathroom.

"Mushrooms," I mutter to myself, "mushrooms in something he's eaten."

Dad comes in shaking his head. "He forgot to check that there weren't mushrooms in the spaghetti sauce."

Marty is allergic to mushrooms and he always gets sick if he eats them.

"I told Mom not to let him eat there," I said.

"Why?" Dad smiles. "Did you know what was on the menu?"

That makes me think. Why *did* I say he shouldn't eat there? I'd just gotten this flash of something bad, I wasn't sure what.

"I'm not sure," I answer Dad. "I just had a feeling."

"Want to watch a little TV in our bed?" Dad offers.

I gladly accept and watch a couple of reruns. Since I don't watch that much TV during the year (except for talk shows after school, of course) I haven't seen them before. My friend Susie comes over and hangs around with me for a while. We try to figure out how many of the female stars on those sitcoms are suffering from some kind of eating disorder. We count at least five, in one hour alone! Susie is a little plump—baby fat, my mom says—but thank goodness she isn't obsessed about it. In fact, the two of us eat like horses all the time.

Finally my eyes start to droop, and even though it's only around eight o'clock I drop off in front of the set.

I have very strange dreams. I keep waking up from them. I get images of a party with balloons and happy faces, and then there's a fortune-teller with a crystal ball and I'm looking into it and I see everyone at the party putting on masks with angry, horrible expressions and they're all screaming at me and then I'm all alone.

I wake up to find that there's a party in the living room—balloons, cards, all my friends from school and BBYO (the Jewish youth group I belong to). Dad lets them stay for a while then throws them all out so I don't get too tired. Probably I had that dream, I think, because subconsciously I heard them setting up the party. Still, the end of the dream stays with me for a while—like I've eaten a bad apple and can't get the taste out of my mouth.

THREE

I START SCHOOL A WEEK LATE. MY NEW HOME-room teacher, Mr. Kratchaw, smiles and tells me he hopes I'm better. And he adds that he hopes I'll have a good year.

"At least someone doesn't seem to mind being here," he says. That surprises me. I mean, usually a teacher wouldn't say that to a student. "Why," I say, "don't *you* want to be here?"

He stares at me all shocked and says, "How did you know what I was thinking?"

"Thinking?" I repeat. "You just said, 'At least some-one doesn't mind being here.'"

Mr. Kratchaw gives me a sceptical look. "I was *thinking* . . ." He laughs nervously. "No, you heard wrong, Jade." He goes back to his desk, muttering.

Of course he said it out loud, I think as I head over to my desk, otherwise how could I have heard it?

But I quickly forget about that conversation because something funny seems to have happened with my vision. As I'm talking to my friend Patti, and she's telling me about all the great parties I missed over the last couple of weeks, I start to see a kind of green light around her. And for some weird reason the light makes me feel like something is wrong with her. I reach out and touch her shoulder.

"Are you feeling okay?" I ask her.

Her face flushes.

"Look, I don't know what Susie told you," Patti seethes, "but Bruce would never hurt me on purpose. He was drunk, okay? And we got into a fight. He just didn't realize how hard he was pushing me."

"Hey, chill," I say. Although I *had* heard rumours about Bruce, and I can tell that she's covering up. "Susie didn't say anything to me."

"Then how did you know?"

"I didn't know. This is the first I've heard about it. Wow, that's *awful*. Are you okay?"

"I'm fine!" she exclaims. "And Susie should butt out! She wants me to report him to the *police*. She should get a life." And then Patti stalks off.

I never liked Bruce. And I'll bet it won't be the last time he gets drunk and pushes Patti around. She should listen to Susie.

I find Susie to tell her all of this when suddenly I see a light around her, too. It's kind of a white, yellow glow and it just makes me feel like she's all happy inside. I blink my eyes over and over so it will go away, but it won't. I get so distracted that I forget to ask her about Patti.

I go home early but I don't tell Mom or Dad about these strange lights. I don't know what to tell them anyway—it's all too weird. I just say I'm tired and they assume that's all it is. Except, when I look at either of them for any length of time I start to see colours around them, too. I can't take it so I go to bed with a book and fall asleep early.

~

My second day at school is even worse than my first. I'm walking down the hall with Susie and Patti, who are barely speaking to each other, when Jason slaps me on the back.

"How are ya doing?"

"Great, fine. How about you?"

"I'm cool."

But when I look at him he doesn't look cool. That weird light thing is happening again, but this time it's not so much light as dark—like he's got some sort of cloud around him or something. And then I get a feeling that this cloud has something to do with Cathy. I try to think back to the gossip Susie's been feeding me. Did she say they'd broken up? She must have, and that's why I'm imagining I can almost *see* his gloom.

"Hey, Jason, it's me," I say. "You don't have to put on a brave face—Cathy was a ditz anyway."

"What are you talking about?" Jason says. "Did Cathy say anything to you?"

"No," I say. I turn to Susie to bail me out. She shrugs like she doesn't know *what* I'm on about.

"I just heard you'd split," I say.

"Well, we haven't," Jason says. "Someone is just making stuff up, as a joke on you probably."

"Yeah," I say, "I guess. Sorry."

"No problem."

Susie and I are sitting in the cafeteria eating when I see Jason actually pushing kids out of his way as he heads toward us. He glares at me, hands on hips, when he gets to our table. "Cathy just broke up with me! You *did* know," he accuses. "She talked to you!"

"She *didn't*," I insist.

"Then how did you know?"

"Honestly, I thought someone had told me," I say. "Someone *must* have told me. I just can't think who it was."

"I thought we were friends," says Jason. "You could at least be honest and tell me who it was."

"I *am* being honest," I object. "I can't remember."

Jason takes a big breath, then looks at me gloomily. "Probably you were so sick you can't remember. It's cool, Jade. Forget it."

"Thanks, Jason," I say. "And don't worry, you'll find someone else."

Jason wanders off and Susie pulls me along to our next class. "Maybe Cathy told you when she was over at the house," she suggests. "At your party. You were still pretty out of it then."

I nod. "That must be it."

But inside, I remember that Cathy and I were never alone—she couldn't have told me. So how did I know?

I spend the rest of the day trying to ignore the strange "feelings" I'm getting when I see or talk to certain people. And trying to blink away the colours I see around them. By the time I get home I'm exhausted. Still, I know that there's a reasonable scientific explanation for everything so I head straight for my computer and bring up *meningitis* in the encyclopedia. Unfortunately it doesn't mention any of the after-effects I'm having. I realize that if this keeps up I'll have to tell someone.

Fortunately I have a doctor's appointment Wednesday morning. I just switched to my parents' doctor this summer; before then I'd gone to a pediatrician. My new doctor treats me like an adult, which I like. She won't discuss anything that goes on between her and me without my permission, so that I'll feel free to totally confide in her—especially about sex, drugs, stuff like that. Except my life is so straight I don't have secrets. I've tried drinking and doing weed of course—but I only do them occasionally, because I really don't want to get into that scene. I've seen the kids that are—they're still so blasted after the weekend they can't think straight for days. I intend to get a scholarship to one of the top Ivy League colleges in the U.S., and they count your marks from grade nine up. I can't afford to lose two or three days a week. Also, I have to admit, I hate being out of control. Sure, I'll have a buzz now and then, but that's about it.

As for sex. Well, of course I could've had sex. Guys will have sex with a watermelon if they're desperate enough. Lots of girls try to prove their love by having sex. It only proves they're having sex. I'm not interested. Well, okay, I take that back. I'm *really* interested, but I haven't gone out with anyone I'd want to do it with. Mom keeps telling me, take it slow, really get to know him. By the time that happens, like in a month or two or three, we've usually broken up. So, there you go. I haven't had any secrets for the doctor.

Until now.

FOUR

"How are you?" Dr. Merano asks me. She's very quiet and calm.

"I've had a few headaches," I reply.

"Let's take a look."

She peers into my eyes with her little light and checks my reflexes. She asks me if I've been dizzy or nauseated. I take a deep breath.

"I'm having a kind of strange after-effect," I say.

"Go on."

"Well, it's really hard to explain. I think there's something wrong with my eyes. I see colours around people, but it's not just that. The colours tell me things." I hold my breath, expecting her to flip, but she doesn't.

"Can you see a colour around me, right now?" she asks, as if what I just said was perfectly normal.

"Yes, it's kind of green yellow."

She nods. "Anything else?"

"I'm getting weird feelings. Sometimes it's almost like I can hear what people are thinking. Sometimes I almost *know* what's going to happen to them."

"Do you know what's going to happen to *you*?" she asks.

That stops me dead. "No," I say, puzzled. "I don't."

"Well, I doubt you've suddenly become a prophet." She smiles. "It could just be that you've been away from your friends for a while and you're very sensitive to their feelings and moods."

"Do you think so?" I say, hoping she's right. "But what about my eyes?"

"Everything looks fine to me. But you did have a very high fever. Let's get a neurologist to check you over, just to be sure."

That seems very sensible to me.

The earliest she can get me in to the specialist is in a week. In the meantime I feel relieved just because I told her and she didn't freak and say I'm going nuts or even seem very worried. I go back to school feeling better.

When we have a spare I go to the library and look up near-death experiences. It turns out there are a ton of books on it—well, three anyway. One is about children and their "NDEs," the other two are just general descriptions.

I start reading, and the more I read the more unsettled I feel. These people describe almost *exactly* what happened to me. Some see angels when they get to the light, others see Christ or some other religious figure, others see dead relatives. *They* all seem to believe that it's more than a dream, and no one can convince them otherwise. I have to admit that the things I felt there, corny-sounding things like pure love, even joy, I'd never felt before. So if it was a dream, how did I dream up feelings I never even knew were possible? Or the light? It was so bright, yet I could see perfectly.

Still, as Mom says, a dream can feel as real as anything. And who knows what emotions are stored in our subconscious?

I'm so entranced with what I'm reading that I forget about my next class, and it's not until Mrs. Morrisette, the librarian, shakes me to tell me school's over that I realize what I've done.

"It's not like you to skip class," she says, looking at me curiously. Teachers never get mad at me. I'm considered a dream student. Everything I do is okay by them.

"Research," I lie, thinking fast. "For a psych project I'm working on."

"Well, check them out and you can finish reading them at home."

Suddenly, it's like I have a thought in my head about Mrs. Morrisette's mother, whom I don't even know! And a feeling that everything will be fine. It is so strong I blurt something out before I can stop myself.

"Don't worry, Mrs. Morrisette," I say, "your mother will be better soon. I'll bet she'll be out of the hospital by next week."

Mrs. Morrisette stares at me. "And how did you know my mother was ill?" she says.

"I can sort of see her in my mind. It feels like she's in a hospital somewhere, but not here in the city. And you don't know whether to go see her and take off from school. But you don't have to."

Mrs. Morrisette blinks and her jaw drops. "Is this some kind of joke, Jade? Because it really isn't funny."

"I'm sorry," I mumble. "Someone must have told me your mother is sick."

"I don't know who that could be," she replies, very puzzled. "I'm sure I haven't told any of the students."

When I get home I try to calm myself down. Someone obviously must have told me about Mrs.

Morrisette's mother, and I forgot when I was sick. And when I remembered it felt like some kind of "vision" thing, but really it wasn't! Maybe Mrs. Morrisette didn't tell any of the students, but another teacher might have mentioned it to one of my friends. There is an explanation for everything, sometimes it just isn't obvious what the explanation is, that's all.

I should be calm after giving myself this little pep talk but I'm not. I'm restless, and I'm the only one home. I go to the phone and call my Baba.

"Hi," I say, suddenly not knowing what to say, but feeling too upset to be alone in the house.

"Hi, sweetheart. How are you?"

"Okay."

"You don't sound okay. Want to come over?"

"Sure."

Baba lives just two blocks away, in a condo development. I walk over and I'm there within ten minutes.

"You look like you've seen a ghost," she says to me.

"No, it's nothing," I say, not wanting to upset her.

"It's something," she says.

"Baba, I don't want to talk about it."

"That's fine, dear," she says. "Come and have a snack." A snack consists of homemade cookies, a fresh fruit salad she'd just made to bring over to me filled with all these fruits I love like papaya, kiwi, and raspberries, and iced tea. I feel much better after stuffing my face.

"You got too thin when you were sick," Baba says.

"Baba," I say, hesitantly, "do you *really* believe you talk to Zaida?"

She nods. "I *do* talk to him."

"But you can't know for sure it's him," I argue. "I mean, it could just be your own mind."

"You mean, I have no proof?" Baba says.

"Right," I agree. "There's no proof."

"Sweetheart, do you love me?"

"Of course I do!" I declare.

"And can you prove that you do?"

I pause. "No."

"So how do you know you love me?"

"I just do. It's a feeling."

"Well, I just *know* that about Zaida."

"But," I object, "that's different. I have my feelings. True, I can't *see* them, I can't *prove* them, I mean, you have a point there . . ."

She nods in satisfaction.

"But," I continue, "it's not something *outside* of me. All you can say is you *feel* like Zaida is with you. It could just be your own mind imagining what he'd say to you—and you know him so well you can even have an imaginary conversation with him."

Baba looks like she is going to say something but suddenly she stops. She considers me for a moment, then says, "You know, Jade, your great-great-grandmother Fannie could talk to spirits and tell the future. It seems to skip a generation. I have some abilities, too, but Fannie was amazing."

"How?"

"She was well known for her 'powers.' But no one thought anything of it then. Most people accepted it. Oh, I'm not saying she wasn't ridiculed at times. Or that sometimes it wasn't a curse seeing ahead that way."

At that point I almost tell her everything but I feel like if I do somehow that'll make it real. And, after all, I don't believe in *any* of this! And nothing is going to change my mind.

FIVE

I'M COMING OUT OF MATH CLASS JUST AS MY friend Zach is going in. Last year we were both in the same class and had fun problem-solving together. This year we're in different classes. I stop him.

"Hey, Zach, want to get together at noon and go over your test?"

"Why?" he says.

"So you can ace it next time!" I reply.

"How do you know I didn't ace it this time?"

"Well, a seventy-five is okay for *most* people but for *you*, Zach . . . !"

"Jade!" He looks really upset.

"What?"

"I never told you what my mark was." His tone is accusing.

"Yes, you must have. You got a seventy-five, right?"

He's really glaring at me.

"I didn't tell *anyone*, Jade. I was too upset. Have you been going through the teacher's papers?"

"Yeah, right!" I reply indignantly. "I wouldn't!"

Ms. Mahon overhears us.

"Zach, did you say Jade went through my papers?"

A crowd is beginning to gather.

"How else would she know my mark?" he growls.

"Jade?"

"I don't know, I just know. I'm *sure* he told me. He must've forgotten telling me."

"I didn't tell *anyone*," he insists.

"Jade?" Ms. Mahon repeats.

"Well, then, it must've been a lucky guess," I say, although my heart is sinking and I'm beginning to realize that it could be one of *those* episodes. How *could* I have known? But this time it was so clear, I can *remember* Zach saying "I got a seventy-five," but maybe he only *thought* it. Or maybe I didn't even pick it up from him, I just *knew*. I shake my head.

"No," I say aloud. "Zach *must've* told me. You know I'd never go through your papers, Ms. Mahon."

She looks at Zach. "There really wasn't an opportunity for her to do that, Zach. Not that I can think of, anyway."

The bell rings for class.

"Everyone break it up," says Ms. Mahon. She moves Zach into the room. He gives me a dirty look over his shoulder. I return it! The jerk. Everyone is staring at me. I feel sick inside. How could that have happened? It wasn't like I got a "feeling" first, the way I did with Mrs. Morrisette and her mother. I was *sure* it was real. And yet, when I think about it, I haven't seen Zach over the last few days. So it was "real," but only in my head. I *am* losing my mind.

I sit in think lab, except I can't think. Not about what's going on in class, anyway. I'm scared. That fever must have scrambled up every neuron in my brain. One thing is for sure—I have to learn to keep my mouth shut. I just won't say *anything* to *anyone* unless I'm positive it's not something my brain is concocting.

Noreen is at the front explaining a problem. Her skin looks yellow. I stare at her. I can feel that she is really sick. She should be home in bed. I am about to say something to her as she passes by but I bite my tongue. I've gotten in enough trouble.

Susie is sitting beside me. She nudges me. "What was all that with Zach?"

"Who knows?" I say. "He was being an idiot. He *must've* told me his mark." But even as I protest to my best friend, I know he didn't.

Noreen puts up her hand.

"May I be excused? I'm not feeling very well."

Mr. Casey nods and waves her out.

How did I know she was sick? No big deal there, I try to convince myself. She looks sick. Probably everyone noticed. I turn to Susie.

"Noreen looks really bad, eh?"

"Does she?" Susie answers. "I don't know, she looks the same to me. You know who she's going out with? Reuben Morris."

"I think both she and Reuben are gonna be out of commission for a while," I whisper.

"Why?"

Oh no. I'm doing it again.

"Nothing," I say. "Forget it."

She kind of cocks her head, the way she does, and pulls her mouth over to one side in a sort of grimace. "If you say so."

I pretend to be engrossed in my work. I keep up the pretence for the rest of the day and finally, it's three-fifteen, we're on the third floor in foods and I'm just *dying* to get home. I'm exhausted from *not* speaking for fear of blurting out the wrong thing. And now some idiot is burning his or her butter tarts.

"Someone's burning something," I call out. A kind of general warning.

Everyone rushes to check their pastries but no one can find the culprit making all the smoke.

Mrs. Lossitt double-checks and then shakes her head at me. "I can't find anything, Jade. Does anyone else smell smoke?"

No one can. It's getting really strong now, and yet Mrs. Lossitt is right, I can't actually see the smoke. But I can smell it, and when I try to focus I realize that I can sort of "see" it in my head. Not real smoke. The image of smoke. And it's coming from the basement. I forget my resolution.

"There's a fire in the basement!"

Everyone in the class bursts out laughing. Even Susie.

Matt yells out, "The fire's in your brain, Jade. Go home and lie down. Or do you wanna guess what all of us got on our math tests?"

Too bad I don't have the power to disappear. Because that's what I really want to do now.

And then the fire alarm goes off. For a second no one moves. They all stare at me.

Matt laughs again. "Bloodhound!" he calls out at me.

I wrinkle my nose and put my hands up like paws and pretend to sniff.

"Ovens off!" Mrs. Lossitt yells. Then everyone files out.

I flick off my oven and Susie and I hurry out into the hall with the others. "I can't smell any smoke," she says, looking at me curiously.

"I've always had a good sense of smell," I say, as loud as possible so everyone hears me.

Matt makes more panting sounds. I play along. I'd much rather they think it is my good sense of smell than have them suspect the truth. That I had a "feeling."

By the time we're on the first floor everyone can smell the smoke and the orderly exit turns into a bit of a panic. But I *know* there's no reason to worry. Sure enough, ten minutes later the bell rings and we're let back into school to go to our lockers and collect our things. The secretary announces over the P.A. that it was just smoke from a science experiment that set the alarms off.

I can't get home fast enough. The trouble is, how many more days like this can I go through?

SIX

I USED TO LOVE SCHOOL. I KNOW THAT SOUNDS totally nerdy but I guess we all love what we're good at and I was good at school. I mean, I'm not the most popular girl and I'm not great at sports, in fact, I basically stink, and I'm not a big party animal. I have friends, though, and we have fun at school. We're called the eggheads 'cause we're all pretty smart, but the name never really bothered us. It still doesn't bother me—after all, egghead is a *way* better name than freak. And, according to Susie, that's what the kids are starting to call me now.

Not only do I talk about things I shouldn't know about, but I also see these colours. According to the books from the library, I must be seeing auras. And now I'm beginning to feel what the auras mean—I can look at someone and know if they're mad or upset.

Those are the easy ones to read. Sometimes, like with Noreen, I can see if someone is sick.

Finally, Wednesday arrives and I go to the neurologist, but he can't find anything physically wrong. So he recommends a shrink. My appointment is for Friday morning.

~

A small man with black curly hair and bright blue eyes greets us in the waiting room. He introduces himself as Dr. Manuel and ushers me into his office. It's nice, but there's no couch. He smiles at me and offers me a chair.

"Now tell me what's worrying you," he says.

"I seem to know what's going to happen to people," I say. "And I see auras around them, too."

"Can you see mine?" he asks, just like Dr. Merano had. They both act like they hear this every day. I mean, isn't this where he's supposed to tell me I need help?

I nod.

"What does it look like?"

Oh, I get it. He's humouring me.

"It's white," I reply.

He nods. "That's good, that's supposed to represent truth."

"Is it?" I say.

"Hmmm. And yellow is healing, I believe, green is intelligence, red is anger . . ."

"You believe in this stuff?" I ask, incredulous.

"Don't you?"

"No! That's why I'm here. I think I'm going crazy."

"You said you know things are going to happen," he says. "Tell me about that."

So I give him some examples of a few of the things that have happened.

"And you've been right every time?" he says.

"Yes."

"So have you considered the possibility that you *are* psychic?"

Did Mom know that she was sending me to a shrink who is nuts himself?

I just stare at him.

"I mean," he continues, "if you *are* psychic, you aren't crazy, correct?"

I don't answer.

"Correct?"

"I guess."

"The important thing here," he says, "is to rule out any serious illness. Let's go over everything step by step."

I tell him everything, from my near-death experience right to Baba and her theory about all this running in the family.

"Maybe you've been given a gift," he says.

I glare at him. "I don't want it! I'm a freak! Just make it go away."

"Is being different so bad?" he asks.

"Yes!"

"Maybe *that's* what we should be dealing with here," he says, "how you can deal with this. How about it?"

"No!" I declare. "I'm not going to talk about how to 'deal' with it, I want you to make it go away."

"I can't," he replies. "But if you feel that it's interfering with your ability to cope, then I can help you with that. Just let me ask you a few questions. Do you feel like people are out to get you, Jade?"

"No, not really. They're just making fun of me."

"Now, you told me you see things other people don't see, and you hear things other people don't hear. Are the things you hear coming from inside you or from outside of you?"

I think about that for a minute.

"Inside, I guess."

"So you don't feel like there's an outside voice or presence trying to control you?"

"No," I answer.

"That's good," he says. "You see, I think that the important thing here is for you to feel comfortable with what you're feeling."

"No," I exclaim, getting really upset. "I don't *want* to feel comfortable with it. I want it to go away! Can't you give me some drugs or something?"

"I could tranquilize you, but I don't believe that would be the best thing for you."

"But I don't want to feel those things!"

"Jade," he says, "I can help you cope with these new feelings. I understand that you're scared but I don't think you're sick."

"I am!" I declare, bursting into tears, and I run out of the office.

Mom and Dad are in the foyer and he calls them in. When they come out they are both shaking their heads. We get in the car and Mom says, "Don't worry, dear, we'll find someone else. I'd heard Dr. Manuel was so good. Do you know what he just said to me? Anything is possible! Well, I don't think *this* is possible!"

As soon as we get home Mom starts to call around and somehow, using her connections I guess, she gets me another appointment for right after lunch. The three of us troop into another waiting room, I sit nervously again and finally an older man, quite tall and thin, calls me into his office.

He asks me a bunch of questions and hardly looks at me. He takes notes and nods and then he gets up and calls in my parents.

"We may have some cause for concern here," he says.

My stomach twists up. *Am* I crazy?

"She *did* have a very high fever. And she seems to be experiencing anxiety connected to her illness. These episodes aren't necessarily psychotic, however. Let's try her on a mild dose of an anti-anxiety drug and see what happens."

Mom seems relieved. But I'm not. Why did he say psychotic? As soon as we get home I look the word up in the dictionary. According to *Webster's*, it means "relating to or suffering from psychosis." I look up psychosis: "Serious mental derangement."

Great. So now I may be deranged!

I pop my first pill. *Anything* to get back to normal.

SEVEN

ROSH HASHANAH, THE JEWISH NEW YEAR, IS early this year, on the twenty-fourth of September. Mom always has the first night here, inviting Baba, Aunt Janeen (her younger sister, who is a TV news producer), and Dad's family. My grandparents on Dad's side are both living full time in Florida now. They often come for the holidays, but this year Grandpa has a bad flu so they've decided to stay put. Dad has a brother and a sister, but one lives in Toronto and the other in Vancouver. Sometimes they fly in as well, but this time it's only us.

Because it'll be so small this year, Mom tells Aunt Janeen to bring her "significant other" and his three teenaged sons. Sahjit and Aunt Janeen have been going out for over a year and I think it's pretty serious. Sahjit is an immigration lawyer and he and Aunt Janeen met when Aunt Janeen was doing a piece on deporting criminals. He's East Indian, Hindu, Mom says, so they don't exactly celebrate the Jewish New Year, but apparently they are very excited about being invited. Of course, basically it's just a dinner. They'd find Passover much more interesting (and more boring for the kids) because we do a whole service before the meal.

I can't be of much help to Mom this time because the pills have made me useless—I drop stuff and fumble. On the other hand they have *definitely* reduced these "feelings" of mine. Although it's not like they've gone, they're just muted, and I can still feel them there in the background. And I feel sleepy a lot and kind of right out of it. I walk around school like a zombie. From freak to zombie. Not much of an improvement.

Mom is using her good china so she's more or less told me to go lie down. Even though I'm all drugged up I can feel, distantly, somewhere inside me that I'm excited about tonight. I decide to skip my before-dinner pill just so I won't feel completely out of it. Susie is coming, of course. She comes to all my holiday things and I go to all of hers. I get to have Christmas at her house, and she has Purim and the others here. Marty's best friend, Jamie, is Jewish so he has to be at his own family dinner. This makes Marty grumpy.

Aunt Janeen arrives looking beautiful and sophisticated, as always. She's medium height with long, naturally curly, reddish hair, big brown eyes, high forehead and cheekbones—she always manages to look stunning. And with her are Sahjit and his boys. I am introduced to the oldest, David, the middle, Jon, and the youngest, Ben. I'm surprised by their names. I thought they'd be exotic Indian ones.

Still, I don't have time to think much about that. Because I'm trying not to stare at Jon, the middle son. He is just too gorgeous for words. I mean, like, movie-star stunning, beautiful, incredible, words cannot describe, drop-dead gorgeous. It takes *all* my willpower not to stay rooted to the spot just staring at him.

He's around five foot ten, slim, with wavy hair and these amazing deep brown eyes, almost black actually, and a full mouth, a dazzling smile, high forehead, high cheekbones.

"You look a lot like your aunt," he says to me.

I can feel myself flushing—I take that as an incredible compliment. Actually, I've been told by a lot of people that I look way more like Aunt Janeen than like Mom or Dad, and Aunt Janeen looks just like Baba did so I guess I take after my Baba.

Mom has put me in between Susie and Jon so we make small talk throughout dinner—school, stuff like that. Marty is happy because Ben is his age and they seem to hit it off right away. Jon is in grade twelve at Pearson High in one of the new suburbs. We live in one of the older areas of the city, River Heights, so I go to Kelvin. I find out that he's a whiz in English—which really impresses me—but he can barely get through his science and math. I offer to help him. I know he's two grades above me but I can understand just about anything to do with math. It's way easier for me to do the practical things that have a right answer and a wrong answer and that's that. I hate it in English when the teacher starts to talk about interpretation.

Since I haven't taken a pill I begin to sense things again. The feeling in the room is good but there is something wrong, somewhere. Or something is about to go wrong. It's so distant, though, that I can't tell who it relates to or what it is, and I just try to ignore it.

I overhear Sahjit tell Baba that he is presently working along with B'nai Brith to file papers to have a war criminal extradited to Austria.

"He lives just over in Crescentwood," Sahjit says. "He was responsible for the murder of an entire town of Jews in the war."

"He's a Nazi?" I ask.

"He was never in the Nazi Party, according to our papers," Sahjit says. "He was chief of police in this Austrian town and happily carried out the Nazi orders to kill the Jews."

A shiver runs down my spine.

"And he's lived here all these years?"

"That's right. Lots of war criminals entered Canada and the U.S. shortly after the war ended. He runs a factory just off Taylor Street."

"That's so creepy." I shudder. After all, if this guy and the Nazis had been in charge in Winnipeg, my Baba and Zaida would have been shot and killed, Mom and Dad would never have been born, or they would have been killed, and I certainly would not be here.

"It's not fair. Even if you do get him sent back and he goes to jail he's lived his whole life in freedom. Did he get married and have a family?"

"He has five kids," says Sahjit.

"Yeah, and I'll bet they all think he's the greatest and *you're* the jerk," I say.

"That's right," Sahjit nods.

"It's disgusting," Jon says, shaking his head.

Isn't he wonderful?

Susie nudges me. "You're drooling," she whispers. I wipe my mouth in horror. She giggles. "Not *really*," she says. She rolls her eyes toward Jon. I nudge her back and glare at her to shut up. It's not that obvious, is it?

~

I've taken my pill and I'm just getting ready for bed when Dad calls to tell me the phone is for me. It's Jon.

"Were you sleeping?" he asks.

My heart sinks. My voice must sound as dopey as I feel. I try to sound bright and cheerful.

"No," I reply.

"Just wanted to say what a good time I had tonight."

"Really?" I pause. "Me too."

"I was wondering." He pauses. "If you'd like to catch a movie over the weekend—or go for coffee?"

"Yeah. Sure."

"Is Saturday okay?"

"Yeah, sure."

"So, think of something you'd like to see."

"Sure, great."

I can't get any other words out of my mouth. I'm completely tongue-tied.

"So, talk to you later?"

"Yeah, sure, later."

"Bye."

"Bye."

I hang up and jump up and down. Yes! I can't *believe* it! A simply gorgeous guy and he's asked me out! Wow! I just wish I could've thought of something to say. Now he probably thinks I'm a complete idiot. Never mind. I'm going off this medicine Friday. I am *not* going to be so doped up I can't talk to him. This is great!

EIGHT

We decide to go for coffee at the Roasting House. We sit downstairs in the non-smoking section and we both order hot chocolate. It's the best hot chocolate in the city. I have a huge piece of chocolate cheesecake and Jon has some kind of really delicious apple thing. I know because he offers me some. So I offer him some of mine. Those eyes. I'm quite sure that I'm completely, totally, completely, in love. I've never felt anything like this before. I spent all of last week dreaming about him. He called me every night. By Wednesday I was actually able to speak more than monosyllables and we started to talk about who our friends are, stuff like that.

The trouble is, I've gone off my medicine and all my feelings are coming back. I can see an aura around Jon.

It's kind of yellow. I *know* he's a good person inside. I can feel it.

He writes poetry. He edits the school newspaper. And he likes Leonard Cohen, so I've been listening to Cohen all week. At first I couldn't get used to his voice but once you do his stuff is wicked. He's Jewish, too. I think that's pretty cool. We talk about our favourite songs of his—mine is the one that goes, "There's a crack in everything, that's how the light gets in." I love that. To me it means, kind of, that nothing's perfect, in fact, things that aren't perfect are okay because that's how the light—meaning life, beauty and truth, and all that—gets in.

I tell all this to Jon and he teases me. "I thought you couldn't interpret things," he says.

"I can't," I say. "Or at least I didn't think I could. You're a terrible influence on me. My parents can't believe I'm listening to Leonard Cohen. Mom says next it'll be Bob Dylan."

"He rocks," says Jon.

"Okay," I sigh, "Bob Dylan next."

"Actually," Jon says, "tomorrow night I'm reading some of my own stuff at the West End." He means the West End Cultural Centre. "These two professors have been putting on these readings. You just have to turn up and sign up and you get to read two poems. It'll be my first time reading in public. I'm sort of scared."

"It's too dangerous," I say, suddenly terrified. "Don't go."

"Only your ego gets hurt," he grins. "Why don't you come?"

"Yeah, I'd love to," I say. "I'll ask. But I really don't think you should go."

He looks at me. "Why not? My poetry is *bad*, but . . ."

"No, no," I say, "I'm sure it's great. I don't know, I just don't think it's a good idea."

He's giving me a weird look. I realize I'm having another one of my "feelings." I'd better shut up or he'll never see me again. But what if, I mean, just what *if* there's something to it? I have to warn him, right? Wrong. After all, it's all nonsense. I change the subject.

We walk home down Corydon. I'm dying for him to take my hand but he doesn't. I think of taking his, but what if he only wants to be friends? That would be too humiliating.

"I'll call you tomorrow," he says once we're home. "This was fun."

"Yeah," I agree, "it was. See you."

I go in floating on air. But when I tell Mom about tomorrow she says that she and Dad have to be out so I have to stay home with Marty. We have a huge fight about it. I hate younger brothers. Why do they even exist? They're like mosquitoes, no use to anyone whatsoever. Of course Marty, who is all of twelve, keeps insisting that he can stay alone, but Mom won't hear of it. Besides, she says I'll have no way to get home, and on and on. I can take a bus home! Not from that area, at that time of night, apparently. Honestly. Parents are just *too stupid* sometimes. I'm fifteen, after all. In some cultures I'd be married with kids already. But then that strong feeling of something horrible happening hits me again and I go and take a pill.

Sunday evening I spend snapping at my brother and trying to do homework, which is really hard when all I feel like doing is dozing in front of the TV. I hate the way these pills make me feel. But I hate the way I feel without them.

Around midnight I wake up with a start. Then the phone starts to ring. Mom and Dad are still out so I have to go answer. It's Aunt Janeen.

"Is your Mom there, Jade?"

"No, they're out at some big fund-raising dinner thing. They'll probably be back soon, though. What's the matter?"

She's so upset she doesn't notice that I've asked her what the matter is before she's even told me something is the matter.

"Is it Jon?"

"Yes," she says, sounding surprised now.

"Is he okay?"

"He was on his way home from this poetry reading, waiting for the bus actually, and this gang attacked him. Called him horrible names. They were skinhead types. He's in hospital, I'm calling from there now."

"Is he okay?" I ask again.

"Yes, sweetheart, he's going to be fine. He may have a cracked rib, he's finding it very painful to breathe. He's got some ugly cuts and bruises and he's going to be sore all over for days. They want to keep him here overnight after they get him cleaned up just to make sure he's not bleeding internally or anything."

"Can he describe who did it?"

"He says they were kids, his own age, maybe a little older, but they wore bandanas over their faces."

Suddenly a face forms in my mind and it's so real I let out a small scream and drop the phone.

"Jade? Jade?"

I can still hear Aunt Janeen's voice. "Jade! Are you all right? What is it?"

I pick up the receiver and close my eyes tight. When I open them the image is gone.

“Even the pills aren’t working,” I mutter.

“Jade, what is it? Is someone there?”

“No, no, Aunt Janeen, no one’s here. I saw a face for a minute . . .”

“Have you been taking your pills?”

“Yes.” Of course the entire family knows about me, but Aunt Janeen swore she wouldn’t tell Sahjit, who might tell Jon. “But they’re not working right now, I guess.”

“Jade, honey, I know it’s not my business—oh, never mind.”

“What?”

“No, nothing. Your mom wouldn’t want me interfering. She knows best, I’m sure. You get to bed. Leave your mom a note and let her know what’s happened. I’ll stay at the hospital.” She pauses. “I hear you two had a good time last night?”

“You heard that?” I say. “From who?”

“From whom, you mean,” she teases me. “Why, from the horse’s mouth. He was disappointed you couldn’t go to his reading tonight. We *wanted* to go but he wouldn’t let us. Said it would be too much pressure.”

But he didn't feel like that about *me*. He wanted me to be there. I find myself smiling and then realize I have no right to be smiling while he's suffering in the hospital.

Then I get mad. What creeps would do such a thing? It's too disgusting. This city used to be a really safe place, just a few years ago. Now suddenly there are all these gangs and shootings—it's gross.

As I lie in bed I get another flash of the face I saw while on the phone with Aunt Janeen. It's a round face, with piggy eyes and a small flat nose and almost no hair. Why am I seeing this? Is it connected to the thugs who beat up Jon? Bullies. Cowards. They can only do stuff like that when there's a group of them and there's no chance any of *them* will get hurt.

I'm still awake when Mom and Dad get home. I get up and tell them about Jon.

"I felt something bad was going to happen," I say to Mom.

"It's just a coincidence, I'm sure, dear," she says. "After all, if nothing had happened you'd have forgotten you ever had that feeling. It's only when our fears actually match up with what really happens that we think we might be psychic. Think how rarely that happens."

"After all, statistically speaking," Dad says, "you're bound to be right *some* of the time."

"I hope it's like that," I say, and I go to bed. Once I would have been sure they were right. Now? Now I'm not sure of anything.

NINE

I GLANCE AT THE CAR. I TURN TO SAY SOMETHING to Marty. And then the car explodes. I wake up screaming.

"Jade, Jade, what is it?" Dad is hovering over me. Mom runs in behind him.

I stare at him. Look around. I'm in bed. It was just a dream. "It was just a dream," I say.

It's early morning, so I stay up. Don't want to go back to sleep.

I've decided to stay off my pills for the next few days, until my next doctor's appointment. I want to go see Jon after school and I can't do that if I'm too medicated to think straight.

~

At school, I open my locker and a square piece of blue paper flutters out. I pick it up.

The Jewish Conspiracy *is not over.*
Who really caused World War II?
Hitler was a great Leader!
Did the Holocaust really happen?
No. It is,
Propaganda *from the Jews to make Hitler look bad.*
Jews *who kill little Christian babies and bake them into their bread.*
Jews *who run the world's banks.*
Jews *who . . .*

I crumple the paper and sag against my locker. I notice that there are blue papers everywhere, falling out of lockers as they are opened. Susie is reading one. She looks up from it, horrified. Without a word I head to the office and dump the piece of paper on the secretary's desk. Ms. Lindsay picks it up, uncrumples it, reads it. She goes kind of pale. She tells me to sit down and she runs to the principal's office. Mrs. Friesen comes out of the office, two bright-red spots on her cheeks. Her hand is trembling.

"Where did you get this, Jade?"

"In my locker."

"It's in everyone's locker," Susie adds. Susie has followed me into the office.

"Jade," says Mrs. Friesen, "this is despicable. I'm going to do everything I can to find out where this came from."

Just after the morning announcements, Mrs. Friesen gets on the PA.

"Some of you have found a disgusting piece of hate literature in your lockers. I want you to know that the police have been called in and we will stop at nothing to find the perpetrators of this act. Also, I'm going to declare this Holocaust Awareness week. I will try to find survivors who will come to the school to talk about their experiences and every class will be required to read at least one book dealing with the Holocaust and World War II. We cannot allow this kind of vicious work to go unanswered. If any one of you has seen or heard *anything* that might help us discover who is responsible, please come forward. That's all."

She still sounds really upset, but I'm glad she's taking it so seriously. That piece of paper made me feel sick. Really sick inside. How could anyone believe such things?

In English class our teacher, Mr. Crossley, suggests a number of books we could read on the Holocaust.

Susie blurts out just what I was thinking. "Why would anyone write that sort of garbage? And they must believe it, or they wouldn't write it. But how could they believe it?"

"These people are terrified," Mr. Crossley says. "They're afraid of everything—unemployment, poverty, the lack of control they feel in their lives. *This* gives them a feeling of being in control. They find a group, more often a few groups, and blame everything on them. Then it's not their own fault that they can't get work, or no one values them, or even that they are mean and violent people. They have been *forced* into those roles by these terrible other people. Perhaps it all stems from fear."

"So they're cowards, basically," Susie says.

"*I* think so," says Mr. Crossley. "The only way they can survive is to feel that they're better than everyone. And they have their little groups, like a cult, where everyone believes the same, and that makes them feel secure and safe."

"I don't care *why* they do it," I declare. "They're disgusting creeps."

Mr. Crossley nods. "You're right, Jade. I'm not making excuses for them, I'm just trying to explain where the behaviour *might* be coming from. And my explanation is probably too simple anyway—sometimes it's a very complex situation that leads to this sort of thing. At any rate, there are no excuses. And if anyone can get to the bottom of it, Mrs. Friesen will."

I feel all these pitying looks all day. There are quite a few Jewish kids at Kelvin, but we certainly aren't the majority. I can feel that everyone feels sorry for us, and kind of embarrassed. Unless they agree with it. I feel some of that, too. A kind of gloating. I don't know exactly who it's coming from but I know it's there. The medication is almost gone out of me now, I haven't taken anything since Friday, and I am starting to get all these "feelings" back again.

After school, Aunt Janeen comes to pick me up to take me over to Jon's house. I feel a little awkward—after all, we've only been out once—but according to Aunt Janeen, who called this morning to say Jon was home, he wants to see me. To see *me*! Yes!

He looks awful. His face is all swollen up and he's sitting on the living-room couch, reclined against some pillows. Now here is a big example of the difference between males and females. If I looked like that I'd rather *die* than have anyone see me. Especially *him*. Jon tries to smile but then explains that smiling makes his cheeks hurt.

I hand him a get-well card I picked out. Aunt Janeen had to practically drag me out of the card store, I was so worried about picking the right one. Aunt Janeen gives him her card and shows him the flowers she's brought. Then she goes into the kitchen with Sahjit to put the flowers in water.

I sit down in a chair by the couch.

"Why did they do it?" I ask.

"'Cause of the colour of my skin," he answers. "That was obvious."

Again, I get a flash of the same face I saw the night before.

"You didn't see them at all?"

"No, their faces were all covered."

"This morning I opened my locker to find a piece of paper saying the most disgusting things about Jews."

"Really," he says. "Like what?"

I repeat some of it.

"I guess you have to be a white Christian in this city to be safe."

"I guess so," I sigh. "I'm really upset. Aren't you? Doesn't it make you mad?"

His answer surprises me. "It makes me sad. More sad than mad. Karma, you know."

"What do you mean?" I ask.

"Karma?" he says. "Well, it means action. And every time you act, that action is burned in your memory. It becomes part of you, and if it's a negative action you have to liberate yourself from it. If not in this life, then in another."

"You mean in the next life the people who did this might lead really miserable lives? Like be forced to analyse poetry their whole lives or something?"

Jon smiles, even though it must hurt. "Something like that."

"Do you believe you'll be reincarnated?" I ask, really curious.

"Of course."

Just like that. Of course. Like of course there's life after death and we all come back over and over.

"Do you ever stop coming back in different bodies?" I ask.

"Oh, yes. When you have finally burnt off all your karmic debt you can stop returning."

Might not be so easy to get him to convert, I'm thinking. Judaism doesn't really believe in reincarnation. At least, I don't *think* it does.

Aunt Janeen comes back into the room. "Do Jews believe in reincarnation?" I ask her hopefully.

"I do," she says, totally surprising me.

"You do?"

"Absolutely. But as you know, Jade, my Jewish beliefs aren't exactly mainstream. I'm kind of a New Age Jew. And I have quite a different belief in reincarnation than the Hindu one. I don't really believe in karma. I think that once you're sorry and you realize, in your heart, that you've been wrong, then you have a clean slate. Because if that's true you *won't* do it again. I don't think we're here to be punished for our past mistakes, just to learn from them. So each time we die we look at our last life and examine it. Then we choose our next life considering what lessons we have to learn and the best way to learn them."

"We choose," I say.

"Absolutely. We choose whom to meet in this life and how we can help each other—we arrange everything."

"If we're smart enough to do all that, why bother getting born? Obviously, when we're spirits we know it all," I object.

"Knowing it is different from experiencing it. Only experience can really teach a soul," she answers.

By now, I've practically forgotten about poor Jon. "But, then, you're saying everything is fixed by us, before we're ever born! Where's our free will?"

"Our free will comes in two places. In the astral plane, when we choose our life, and in this life, too. We don't have to follow our chosen path. Then we'll learn other lessons. Now if you want a more traditional Jewish answer you'd better ask your Baba or a rabbi. You know enough about Judaism to realize that most Jews don't believe this. Jewish belief is much more about *doing* than believing. It doesn't matter much what you believe as long as you do good."

"Doing is at least practical," I say. "That's what I've always liked about Judaism. Your idea sounds like a good excuse for all the rotten things that happen. Oh, we're just all learning. Maybe I don't want to learn."

Aunt Janeen looks like she's going to say something, then stops herself. Carefully, she picks her words.

"It's hard to explain people having special powers if there isn't a higher source. After all, say, for instance, you could predict the future like some psychics. How could you predict it, if it wasn't already fated?"

I stare at her and feel like strangling her. For an aunt she can be very annoying. She's always been like that. She didn't give away my secret but she almost did. And then, I have to admit, she has a point. But there *must* be another answer. A reasonable, scientific, logical answer. There must be, and I'm going to find it!

"You look upset, Jade," Jon says.

"So do you believe that Jon was meant to get beaten up?" I shoot back at Aunt Janeen. "Is he supposed to *learn* something from it? Are the guys that did it supposed to learn something? Because," I say, feeling furious with her, "it was no accident. They meant to get *him*. They had a reason. And it wasn't just because he was some East Indian kid!"

The room is dead quiet. Sahjit has joined us and they are all staring at me.

"How do you know that?" Sahjit asks.

I dart a glance at Aunt Janeen. She can tell I didn't mean to blurt that out. And I didn't. It just came out. I don't even know why.

"I don't," I stutter. "I just suddenly felt . . . I don't know, sometimes I get these feelings . . ."

Aunt Janeen jumps in. "Jade is just very sensitive and hates to see anyone get hurt. She won't even kill a spider, will you, Jade?"

Actually, I love killing spiders. Jon strikes me more as the type that wouldn't hurt the tiniest life form. But I can see she's trying to get me out of this mess.

I nod. "Right. Sorry. Just upset."

"We all are," says Sahjit, and he pats my shoulder.

When he touches me I suddenly *know* that he too is in danger. I see a grey cloud all around him, and I can feel pain all over—but it's not me that's in pain, it's him. And then the cloud turns almost black and the pain goes away. I feel death. My skin starts to crawl. What should I do? Should I warn him? Should I tell him about my feeling?

But what can I say without giving away the fact that I've turned into a nut? And I'm *not* going to let on about that to Jon. Not in a million years. He's just getting to maybe, possibly, like me. All I need to do is tell him that I *can* see the future.

No. I can't. It's just some weird, strange coincidence, some neurons misfiring in my brain, and maybe, maybe, it'll go away. If I believed in God I would definitely pray to Him/Her to make it go away. Fast.

TEN

BEFORE I GO TO SLEEP I DEBATE WITH MYSELF about whether or not to go back on my medicine. What a choice—either all these "feelings" and "visions" or no feelings except those of being dopey and sleepy. Freak or Zombie. I wonder if I should go back to see Dr. Manuel. He didn't think I was crazy. He didn't think I needed drugs. He wanted to help me accept things. Maybe that's what I need to do.

But I can't. I can't accept it. Because doesn't that mean I have to rethink *everything*? God, death, fate, everything? It's too much. I close my eyes, put on the Mean Bees, and fall asleep to their relentless beat.

I see a car. It's grey. And then a huge explosion. And screams.

I wake up covered in sweat.

~

I sit in class as we discuss *The Diary of Anne Frank*. I guess what I have to deal with is nothing compared to what happened to her. Hidden away like that, always knowing that at any time she and her family could be captured. And then finally the moment of terror arrives, they're discovered and dragged off to a concentration camp. Oh, I forgot. There weren't really concentration camps. Six million Jews didn't really get murdered—one and a half million of them children. I would've been killed. Just because I'm a Jew. For no other reason. What kind of a world is that? What kind of a God is that?

One minute I am staring at a picture of Anne Frank, the next an image of Sahjit fills my head. And with the image comes a feeling, almost like pain, like my whole body *hurts*. Somehow the pain is connected to this image of Sahjit. He's in pain or he's going to be. And then a thought forms in my head: *Stop it. Stop.* The word *stop*.

I bolt out of my chair. Mr. Crossley looks at me.

"Jade? Are you all right?"

"I, I need to make a phone call."

He nods.

I race down the hall to the office.

"I have to use the phone!" I say to the secretary when I get there. "It's an emergency." I don't know his number so I call Aunt Janeen on her cell phone.

"Aunt Janeen, you have to warn Sahjit. Something bad is going to happen to him."

"What do you mean?"

"I don't know! Just something bad!"

"Sweetie, I can't just call him up and tell him that. What's he supposed to *do*?"

"I don't know!" I realize she's right. Should he stay put? Is the danger inside, outside? I try to listen to the feeling, but I don't know how, and anyway it's probably all nonsense.

"Aunt Janeen, I'm sorry," I say. "I'm sure it's nothing. Just ignore it."

"No, I can't ignore it," she says. "Thanks, sweetie." And she hangs up.

The phone is ringing when I get home. It's Aunt Janeen.

"You saved his life."

"What?"

"I called him at the office and told him you'd had a kind of premonition that he was in danger. He was just walking out when I phoned. He had an appointment with this war criminal's lawyer. We talked for a while about what to do." She pauses. "Jade, I don't want to upset you but—as we were talking there was this terrible explosion and his car blew up. If I hadn't called, he certainly would've been in the car."

I sink into a chair.

"Jade? Are you there?"

"It's just—I've been dreaming about a car blowing up. A grey car."

"His car was blue. But you got the blowing up part right."

"This is too crazy. It's like we're in some gangland New York or something"

"Yeah," says Aunt Janeen. "Except here we are, with drive-by shootings, gang beatings, and now cars blowing up! The only difference between us and a big city, I guess, is that here it doesn't happen very often."

"But it's happened to two members of the same family," I point out. "Don't you think that's an odd coincidence?"

"Yes," she agrees, "very odd. I'm going to pull in some favours at the police department and see what they've got. And make sure they have a look at the police report on Jon's attack. Maybe there is a connection." She pauses to think. "Sahjit *was* on his way to see the Nazi war criminal's lawyer. Still, I can't see some eighty-year-old man planting a bomb in Sahjit's car."

"No," I say, "but he could have hired someone to do it."

She thinks for a minute.

"That he could, oh little niece of mine, that he could," she says. "Are you all right? You sound a bit shaken up yourself."

"It's just that I don't understand these feelings and—they scare me."

"I know, sweetie. But maybe it's an incredible gift you've been given. I know I'll always be grateful."

"And what about Sahjit?" I say. "Won't he think it's all too weird—when he has time to think about it. I mean, that I got a 'premonition.' And he's sure to tell Jon!"

"Listen, Jade," Aunt Janeen says. "I've had to tell Sahjit a little about your new abilities."

"Aunt Janeen!"

"I *had* to. When you made that comment the other night, he picked up on it right away."

"But he'll tell Jon! Has he told Jon?"

"No. And he doesn't intend to. He says it isn't his place to tell Jon—that it has to be up to you."

I let out a sigh of relief. "Well, that's *something* I guess." I think for a minute, then I say, "I was able to change what was going to happen. So that must mean everything isn't fated."

"You're right," Aunt Janeen says. "Unless you were *fated* to change it. But I never said everything was fated. That's your Baba's department. That's what she believes. Gotta run. We can discuss philosophy later."

I hang up the phone. It may be philosophy to her, but to me it's my life.

~

Susie and I are on our way to my favourite class, math. Now that I'm off my medicine I can enjoy it again. In fact, it's the only place in school where I feel good any more. At lunch it's a nightmare. Kids snicker and make jokes. Only Susie has stuck by me. She doesn't know what to make of any of this, but I'm her friend and she's not going to drop me. So she says. All my egghead friends think I've gone off the deep end and that I'm behaving "irrationally." The awful thing is that if this were happening to one of them, I'd feel the same way. Stay away. She's lost it. The favourite joke as people pass me now is to throw their hands in the air and yell "Fire!"

Suddenly I see the face. For a minute I'm not sure

whether it's real or in my head so I stop and blink my eyes. It's real, all right.

"What're you staring at?" the guy growls at me.

He's about five foot eleven, real wide, no neck, all bulging muscles, shaved head, and a tattoo on his arm. Some kind of skull and crossbones.

Susie and I just walk on, I don't answer him. My heart is pounding in my chest.

"I've *seen* him," I whisper to Susie as we head to class. "I've seen him in my head, like some kind of vision or something."

"You've probably just seen him here," Susie says. "I have. What a creep."

"That's probably it," I agree, relieved. "I mean, I probably saw him but didn't notice him *consciously*, and then when Jon told me about getting beaten up and I picked up that hate stuff, it was like—well—he is the *most* likely guy, isn't he?"

"He sure is," Susie says nervously. "Maybe we should mention his name to Mrs. Friesen."

"I'm sure she's keeping a close watch on all the skinheads," I reply.

It's a beautiful fall day so after class Susie and I decide to walk home rather than take the bus. I actually get a feeling that I shouldn't, but it's so stupid, I refuse to listen. I meet Marty at the corner of his school, and I get a stronger feeling of trouble so I'm glad I'm with him, but then I remind myself it's all nonsense anyway. We say goodbye to Susie on Ash and walk to Cordova together. There's a park just across the street from our house so we cut across it to get home. Just by a group of trees, the skinhead from school steps out and blocks our way.

"Hey, little Yid. This your little Yid brother?"

At first I don't know what he means. I've never been called a bad name like that before, and it takes a minute to register that Yid might mean Yiddish or something about our being Jewish.

"Hey, I'm talking to you."

I grab Marty's hand and we try to run around him but he's fast for someone so huge and he stops us.

"It's not polite to not answer when you're asked a question. This your brother?"

I clutch Marty's hand. "Yes."

"Now, was that so hard?"

"Let us by," I say.

"I don't feel like it," he says, moving closer, till I can smell his tobacco breath on me. "You think you're too good for me, don't you?"

"Leave her alone!" Marty says.

I look around. There must be someone nearby who can help me. But the place is deserted. I stare at him, he's so ugly, and suddenly, I can *see* things, see things about him. My mind is flooded with images.

"Why don't you go back to your family?" I say. "Your five sisters all miss you."

His eyes widen. "How'd you know about my sisters?" he says.

"I can see them. And your mom can't do the farm work without you. You never should've come here to live with your uncle. He's a bad influence."

The skinhead starts to back away from us. He's gone pale, almost green.

"I told nobody about my family," he whimpers. "You tied in to the police or something?"

"No," I say, "I can *see* things. I'm a *witch*!"

Sweat starts to pour from his forehead.

"You, you, just stay away from me," he says, and then he turns and runs.

Marty is staring at me.

"How'd you do that?"

"I don't know." My knees start to feel like they're going to fold, my heart is thudding in my ears.

"You don't look so good," Marty says. He seems quite unaffected by the entire episode.

"I don't feel so good," I say. And Marty, his hand still clamped onto mine, drags me home.

ELEVEN

I SIT ON MY BED, SHAKING FROM HEAD TO FOOT. Mom and Dad aren't home yet and Marty is on the phone telling all his friends what just happened. He's more excited than scared. I don't have the energy to stop him. And what difference would it make? Everyone at school thinks I'm insane anyhow.

I'm beyond scared. How *did* I see those things? And they were true. *And* they probably saved both Marty and me from something very nasty. I can't seem to stop shaking. I'm freezing cold.

I take a deep breath. Something happened to me when I got sick. I have to face it. But it's not fair. All I did was go to bingo, and because of a chance thing like that I caught something, and now I'll never be the same again. My life will never be the same again.

Nothing will ever be the same again. I start to cry. And I can't seem to stop.

I'm still crying when Mom and Dad come home. Marty tells them what happened and they try to comfort me as if I'm upset because of the skinhead. I'm crying so hard I've begun to hiccup and I can't catch my breath. Mom forces me to take one of my pills and she tells me she's calling the shrink.

"No!" I manage to get out.

"Why?"

"I, I . . . I don't want to see him." I hiccup and sob some more. "Dr. Manuel," I manage to spit out. "I want to see Dr. Manuel."

Mom calls Dr. Manuel and I don't know what she tells him but he apparently suggests that she bring me in now. He was about to go home but he'll stay late.

I'm still sobbing uncontrollably as Mom and Dad lead me to the car and drive me over to Dr. Manuel's office, which is only about five minutes away, just off Corydon. The pill is starting to take effect but I keep crying, only I'm not shaking as much. Mom drives and Dad sits in the back, his arm around me, and he keeps telling me that everything is going to be all right, that I'm going to feel better soon. But he doesn't understand, I'm never going to get better, this is it! This is it!

They propel me into Dr. Manuel's office and he sits me on a chair with a box of Kleenex. He pulls another chair up and sits opposite me.

"Hi, Jade," he says. "Would you like your Mom and Dad to stay?"

I shake my head, no. I don't want them here. They keep looking for some logical reason for all this and so do I and it's not helping. I don't look at them as they leave.

He waits a minute. I keep crying.

"Had a rough day today?" he says.

I nod.

"Can you tell me about it?"

I tell him, in between sobs, what happened with the skinhead. And then I tell him about Sahjit and the car, and the dreams, and about Jon, and after a while I'm not crying any more, I'm just blabbing my head off.

He gets up when I'm finished and brings me a can of cola from a little fridge he has in the corner. I gulp it down.

"Why are you so upset *now*?" he asks, finally.

"Because I realized that something *has* happened to me. I *can* see things other people can't see. It's just—I never believed people could have such powers, so when it happened to me I couldn't accept it."

"But you can now?"

I start to cry again. "What choice have I got?"

"Jade, I know this is hard for you. But accepting this is the first step."

"But what does it *mean*?" I wail.

"Jade," Dr. Manuel says, "look at the drink in your hand."

I do.

"Does it seem real to you?"

I nod.

"You know that it's a red can, with black writing, and bubbly black liquid inside, right?"

"Right."

"What if we gave that can of cola to an iguana. What do you think the iguana would see?"

I think for a minute. "Probably not a can of cola."

"Quite right." Dr. Manuel grins. "And a whale would see it differently than a bird and a monkey would interpret it differently than a mosquito. So what does that mean? Is that can of cola the way you see it, or could it be all those different things?"

I stare at it. "I'm not sure."

"You see, everything we see around us we assume is reality. But Jade, there *is* no fixed reality. All you have in your hand is a bunch of atoms. It's no more solid than the air. If you could look inside your body with a big enough microscope you'd just see atoms, atoms swimming around in a vast space, an inner universe—ninety-nine percent of the human body is empty space. Everyone and everything in the world is made up of the same energies flowing between us all. For instance, our thoughts and feelings—the things we think aren't 'real' because we can't touch them—they're as real as that drink in your hand. Can you see the radio waves that bring you the sounds of radio?"

"No."

"Maybe your system is picking up thoughts and energies that are swirling around you, maybe you're just tuned in to what is invisible to the rest of us. That doesn't mean, though, that it isn't real, that it doesn't exist."

"But I can see the future," I say.

"On the subatomic level, Jade, there is no linear time. Everything happens simultaneously. We humans make linear time. So you aren't seeing the future. You're seeing the moment, the moment we all live in, where past, present, and future all live together. Eternity, for lack of another word. And Jade, I know you love science and math. Well, guess what? All these ideas I've just described to you are theories developed by quantum physicists."

"Really?"

"Really. This isn't nutty New Age stuff, Jade. In fact, this is a field that you could study as you advance in university. Right now at Princeton University scientists are proving that, just by *thinking*, human beings can affect the way machines operate. How is that possible? Because we're all, even machines, made up of the same atoms. Our energies are interacting all the time. The subjects in this study can influence machines thousands of miles away."

For the first time I feel a stirring of hope. Then this isn't all just me being crazy? It's something I could study and maybe, with my gifts, even go further than other scientists have!

"With your gifts," Dr. Manuel says, "you could probably develop this further than other scientists have!"

I start to laugh. He grins. "What did I say?"

"I just had that thought."

"Why doesn't that surprise me?" he says.

That makes me laugh even harder.

"Do you want to go off your medicine?" he asks.

"Yes," I say. "I mean, I took myself off it, and that's

when all this started to happen. So I don't know."

"Do you think you can handle all the things you'll see and feel once you're off it?"

"I don't know," I repeat.

"That's honest," he says. "None of us know what we can handle until we try. The important thing is that you aren't running away from it any more. Running is *much* harder than facing something. That's probably why you finally broke down."

He's right. Suddenly, I feel almost peaceful. And I know that's not just because of the pill I took.

"There's a saying," Dr. Manuel continues, "that we're dealt a certain hand in life—we have no say in that—but we can choose how to play it."

I still have lots of questions. Who deals us the hand? How many of our choices are real and how many are already fixed? Stuff like that. But I don't say anything. My head is still swirling with what he just said, and I'm tired and I want to go home.

On the way to the car Mom assures me that she and Dad love me and it doesn't matter if I can see things.

"But you don't believe in any of it," I say.

"No," Mom corrects me. "I believe *you*. I simply think there is a physical explanation, one we don't yet understand."

"Maybe the physical world is just an illusion," I say, trying out Dr. Manuel's theory.

"Maybe," she says, "but it's all we've got."

"What if it's not all we've got?" I ask.

"That would be nice," Mom answers. "I just don't believe it. Hey," she says, changing the subject, "how about a gelato?"

Our favourite gelato place is only a few blocks away on Corydon. I can already taste what I'm going to have—pistachio and peach.

So we go and pig out on gelato and I have to admit that, for a bunch of atoms, it sure tastes good.

TWELVE

THIS TIME THE HATE MAIL GETS DELIVERED. I SEE it because Marty and I bring in the mail when we get home from school—Mom and Dad won't be home for an hour or so. And it's addressed to me.

Jews kill little babies so they can
drink their blood on the Sabbath.
For centuries this horrible practice has
been going on unchallenged but it is
time for civilized people everywhere
to put a stop to it, to put a stop to them.
A Jew is no better than an infected rat.
What do we do with rats? We cannot let
them run free infecting the rest of us.

I know who's doing this. I can see his face as soon as I touch the paper. I can feel his hatred.

As soon as Mom gets home she calls the police. The sergeant at the desk says they've been flooded with calls—somehow this garbage has been mailed to just about everyone at Kelvin, leading them to believe that someone got hold of the school's mailing list. Mom had already reported our little incident with the skinhead to the principal, Mrs. Friesen, this morning. The guy's name is Roger, apparently, and he decided not to show up at school today. He's eighteen, in grade twelve, having flunked numerous courses.

"If you can't get love, get power," Mom suggests.

"What do you mean?" I ask.

"Simply," she replies, "that people need something to make them feel special. And if they can't get love, in a healthy way, sometimes they'll substitute power for love by joining a gang, or a group like this that binds them in a common cause—whatever the cause is. Hating someone else or everyone else is an effective way to feel part of a group, to feel you belong, to feel superior and more powerful than everyone else. Whoever wrote this has probably been recruiting kids in your school."

There's a creepy thought. Recruiting people so

they'll think and act like him. It reminds me of this old film I saw, *Higher Learning*, about how a kid gets sucked into this neo-Nazi group. Some geeky kid who couldn't fit in . . .

The phone rings and it's Jon. He wants to know if I feel like going out for coffee.

"If you're home by ten o'clock," Mom cautions, when I ask.

I say, "Sure, I'd love to."

We go back to the Roasting House. He's driving his dad's car so we have more time to sit and talk. But I still don't want to tell him what's going on in my life, and since that's all I can think about, at first it's hard to know what to talk about. I *do* tell him about Roger, except I leave out how I got away from him, and I tell him about the hate mail. He's totally disgusted and he starts to tell me about all the crap he's had to put up with growing up with dark skin in a white-skinned world. It's a wonder he has a kind thought for anyone, but he does. And we actually talk about some normal stuff—teachers, friends.

And then, Roger walks past the window.

"There he is," I say.

"Looks like a really nice guy," Jon comments, eyebrows raised.

"Let's follow him," I hear myself saying.

"Are you crazy?" Jon says. "If he notices us we're dead!"

"He's walking. We're driving. Why should he notice us?" I point out. "Hurry up or we'll lose him."

I don't know what makes me want to do it but for once I don't fight the feeling. I grab Jon's hand and pull him out of the coffee shop.

"Does he look like one of the guys that beat you up?" I ask.

"He could be," Jon answers. "He's about the right build—there aren't too many guys like that around."

"No neck," I say.

"Right. No neck."

We hop into his car, which is parked farther down the street, but we easily catch up to Roger as he walks, hands in pockets, down Corydon. He turns down Lilac and walks until Warsaw. There he's greeted by an old man at the door of a big three-storey frame house. Others are arriving too. We drive by, then Jon parks quite far down the street.

I look at Jon. "That old guy couldn't be—"

"My dad's Nazi?" Jon replies.

"Yeah."

"Dad showed me a picture of him. I'm pretty sure it is."

"So maybe there *is* a connection between what happened to you and to your dad," I say. "What's the guy's name?"

"Klaus Schmidt."

"So maybe Klaus had Roger beat you up and even plant that bomb."

"Maybe," Jon says. "Why don't we go over to the police station?"

"There's nothing illegal about a few friends getting together," I point out. "Of course, if we could see what they're doing."

"Jade. No way," Jon says. "We're lucky we haven't been noticed here."

"Come on," I urge him, not even understanding myself why I want to do such a stupid thing. "We'll just see if we can peek in a window, see what they're up to."

"And if they see us?" he says. "His two favourite people—a Jew and an Indian."

I'm out of the car before he can say anything else. It's around eight-thirty now and getting dark fast, but I can see that everyone has moved from the front porch into the house. I slowly walk down the street, Jon right behind me, muttering objections all the way. Before he can stop me I sprint up against the side of the house. It's all dark on this side, though, so I go around to the other side where there are lights on, and a window is open.

We can hear voices, something about a campaign, success, and then there's a dog barking. A big loud dog by the sound of it, getting close to us from somewhere inside the house. This time Jon grabs my hand and pulls me to the back of the house, then into the lane. We hear voices behind us, obviously looking for the cause of the dog's barking. We run down the length of the lane, then back to the street where the car is parked. We leap in and Jon drives away, hopefully without them seeing us.

"Happy?" Jon pants.

"Yeah," I reply. "At least we know that those two are connected and that they're up to something. Now we just have to find out what that is."

"We have to tell the police," Jon says.

"I think we should tell your dad," I suggest. "He'll know whether the police can do anything."

"Want to come to my house?" Jon asks.

"Sure." I think about the feeling of blackness that

came over me when Sahjit touched my shoulder.

"I guess your father has a lot to deal with right now," I say.

"Well, getting your car blown up doesn't exactly make you feel secure."

"Must be awful for you," I sigh. "You worry about him a lot, don't you? But keeping what's happening to Ben from him might not be the best thing."

Jon jerks his eyes away from the road, onto me. "What do you mean?" he says.

"Ben," I reply, "and his friends, smoking up all the time."

"I didn't tell you that," Jon says. "I'm the only one who knows. Even David doesn't know."

My heart almost stops. I *hate* it when this happens. At least when I get a "feeling" I know it's a "feeling" and I can say something, or not. But this is just like with Zach and his math—the "feeling" must be so strong, so real, that I'm *positive* it's something someone has already told me. As Dr. Manuel says, it *is* as real to me as if he'd spoken it.

I'm completely panic-stricken. What do I say? How do I explain this? I try to bluff it out.

"You told me the other night," I say. "You must've, otherwise how would I know?"

"It's not like we go to the same school," Jon says. "Then you'd know just because it's no big secret."

"Maybe that's it!" I say, grasping at anything. "One of his friends who goes to Kelvin probably told me."

"He has no friends at Kelvin."

"As far as *you* know. Hey, I bet you don't know everything about him."

This is horrible. I'm practically lying to him, and he can tell. But I *can't* tell him about me, he'll get spooked, he'll think I'm a freak, he'll be afraid I'll be reading his mind, which I *am*. It's impossible!

He gives me a strange look and we drive in silence until we get to his house.

It's one thing for me to accept myself, but how do I get others to accept me? Answer *that* one, Dr. Manuel—if you can.

THIRTEEN

SAHJIT IS SITTING IN FRONT OF A SMALL STATUE, with incense burning. He's praying.

Jon and I go into the kitchen to wait.

"Do you always pray at home?" I ask. "Don't you go to a temple or something?"

"No," Jon answers, "we have most of our rituals at home."

"Mom says Judaism used to be like that," I comment. "I mean, priests did the animal sacrifices and stuff but there weren't rabbis who had synagogues like now. She said that rabbis were learned men who really knew the Torah. They've only become the heads of synagogues since the Romans destroyed the Temple in Jerusalem."

"If you want to talk to God," Jon says, "you don't need anyone to help you do it."

“Do you believe in God?” I ask. “I mean, is there someone or something out there directing your reincarnation?”

“Yes, I believe in God,” he replies. “But maybe I don’t see God the same way you do. We call God the Brahman—that’s the unknowable divine outside of us—and the divine within us we call the Atman. We make our own karma, and we have to purify it ourselves, with help from the divine.”

I wonder if Hindus believe in psychics.

“Hi.” It’s Sahjit.

Quickly we tell him what we’ve discovered.

“I’ll tell the police, of course,” he says. “But there’s no law against the two of them knowing each other or going to a meeting. And without more than a vague suspicion we’ll never get a warrant from a judge to search the house. That’s probably where they’re printing the hate mail.”

The phone rings. Sahjit answers it and he listens, then looks really upset and slams down the receiver.

“Another one?” Jon asks.

Sahjit nods.

And they change the subject. Well, I don’t need my “special powers” to figure out that there was someone on the other end of the line, saying nasty things. Put that together with the bomb and Jon's beating and I can see that this family is really in danger. The atmosphere is pretty bad after the call so I suggest to Jon that I'd better get home.

When I do, the phone is ringing. I run to answer it, thinking it's Susie phoning right at ten to see how the evening went.

"Hello?"

At first there is silence.

And then horrible sounds of screaming, as if someone is being tortured. No words, but I know it's meant as a threat—this is what you'll get one day. It makes me feel like throwing up.

I check the call display on our phone, but it's showing "private number."

I slam down the receiver and call Mom and Dad. Dad calls the police immediately and they say they'll contact the phone company in the morning to see if there's anything they can tell them.

~

I walk down the hall at school with Susie and I'm flooded with images. I can see colour around *everyone* today, my medicine having totally worn off, and if I stop, even for a second, and concentrate on someone I can almost see pictures around them of various scenes in their lives.

I'm so busy looking around that I don't notice him until he's standing in front of me. Roger. I step to one side to get around him; he steps too so I can't get by. I step the other way; he mirrors me. I'm just about to call to a teacher when he leans over and whispers in my ear so Susie can't hear.

"No one can help you. No one can protect you every minute of the day."

I shove him away and he takes off. I look for a teacher, but I end up telling Susie instead.

"You have to tell Mrs. Friesen," she says, looking pretty shaken up, so we head for the office.

Mrs. Friesen calls Roger to the office.

"Jade says that you threatened her, Roger."

"Does she?"

"Yes."

"Well, that's what *she* says. She doesn't like me."

"*I* don't like *you*?" I say.

"Do you?" he says, leering at me. I don't answer.

"Well, this isn't getting us anywhere," Mrs. Friesen says. "Roger, I know about what happened in the park. I will call the police if you harass Jade, is that clear?"

Roger grins, as if she's just awarded him a medal or something. "Sure."

"You can go," she says, and he leaves, giving me a wink as he does.

Mrs. Friesen shrugs. "I'm sorry, Jade. I believe you. Frankly, at this point the police can't do much and I'm sure Roger knows it. I wish I could do more."

"I understand," I say.

"Well, I don't!" Susie exclaims. "That guy is a creep. He's dangerous. Does he have to *hurt* Jade before anyone can do anything?"

Mrs. Friesen doesn't answer. Susie and I look at each other. What Susie just said is probably true.

"Please don't hesitate to come to me," Mrs. Friesen says, "if there is *anything* I can do."

"I will," I say.

Susie and I leave the office.

"Roger's involved in all of this, I know he is," I mutter. "And the police can't stop him, Mrs. Friesen can't do anything, so I'm going to have to."

"What are you going to do?" Susie asks, looking worried.

"I'm not sure yet," I reply. "But I'm not going to sit and wait for him to blow me and my family up the next time we get into a car! If no one else can do anything, then I will."

~

I am walking. I see a car, a grey car. This doesn't worry me, but suddenly there is an explosion. People are screaming, there's blood and bodies everywhere, sirens are wailing.

I wake up.

"What is it, honey?" Dad is sitting on my bed.

"That dream," I say hoarsely, "the dream about the car."

"You're just upset because of Sahjit's car," Dad says.

"Maybe," I mutter.

It takes me a long time to fall asleep, though, after that. I think long and hard about what I can do about Roger and his friends.

~

At lunch hour, I go to the shops room where we do electrical work and ask permission of Mr. Hodges to work on some stuff for myself. He agrees, and he even says I can take the equipment home if I promise to return it, or pay for any damages that might happen outside the school.

As soon as I get home I call Jon.

"Can you get the car tonight?"

"Maybe. Why?"

"I want to check out the house on Warsaw again. It's better if I'm in a car."

"What's the plan?"

"I'll tell you when I see you. Is eight o'clock okay?"

"I'll try. If there's a problem I'll call you."

I hang up, then go into the basement with my equipment. I have the entire basement set up with a huge worktable and lots of room for the science experiments I do. Marty also has a portion of it for his video games.

"What're you working on now?" he sighs.

"Nothing," I reply. "Just a school project." If I tell Marty, he'll tell Mom and Dad. They'll forbid me to do this, saying it's way too dangerous. But I think it's more dangerous to do nothing.

Marty turns away, uninterested.

And I bend over my work. They want proof? I'll get them proof.

FOURTEEN

MOM AND DAD PUT UP QUITE A FIGHT ABOUT my going out again tonight. Dates are for weekends, they say. School nights are for homework or hanging out with friends.

"Jon *is* a friend," I say. "And I've been working since after school."

They relent finally, but I can see they are still pretty puzzled and upset. I mean, here is their daughter who's never given them a moment's worry, and not only does she claim she can "see" things, but she's not listening any more, she's getting stubborn, insisting on her own way—behaving like a teenager! Actually, I think it's good for them. They've had it far too easy up until now. Even this, compared to the stuff most of the kids at school go through with their parents, is nothing.

Just before Jon comes the phone rings and I go answer it. I check the call display first—private number. My heart starts to beat a little faster. I pick it up.

"Hello."

"You won't be around much longer. Your whole goddamned race is going to have to go to make it safe for—"

I hang up.

No one is around. Mom and Dad are both upstairs. I don't say anything. I can hear Jon knocking at the door. I race to answer, yell goodbye, grab the bag I've left by the door, and hustle him out to the car.

"I just got another call from our friends," I say. "But we're going to fix them."

"What are you up to?"

"I've made a mike," I tell him.

"A what?"

"A microphone. But one that can pick up just about anything. Like a spy mike."

"Wow. How'd you do that?"

"Well," I admit, "I didn't actually make it. I just modified the equipment that was already in the shops room."

Jon is glancing at me as he drives like he's pretty impressed. But then his expression changes. "What're you going to do with it?"

"Put it against the house," I say. "We can't stand there listening or the dogs will sense us. But they won't sense this."

"They'll sense us putting it there, though," Jon objects.

"All we need to do is place it near the smallest crack in one of those basement windows," I say. "It can pick up anything. We'll let it run for an hour, then go get it. And we'll have our proof!"

"Unless our friends are baking cookies for the poor tonight," Jon says.

"Yeah," I grin, "or out helping new immigrants."

Jon parks at the end of the street again. This time no one seems to be going into the house. Of course, I should have thought of that. It could be weeks before they all come back again. Still, we're here, and I figure it's worth a try. We scurry into the back lane and find the house from there. All seems quiet. I check out the basement windows until I find one slightly open. The dog starts to bark. I turn on the recorder, press record, and we run back down the lane.

"Now what?" asks Jon.

"Hot chocolate?" I suggest. "On me."

We walk over to the Roasting House and sit there, sipping our drinks.

"Do you think it's the same group after both our families?" I ask Jon.

"I wouldn't be surprised."

"But don't you think that's a weird coincidence? I mean, why us?"

"Well, it *could* be just a weird coincidence. They go after Dad because he's trying to get rid of their leader, they go after you 'cause you're a Jew."

"There are lots of other Jews they could go after," I comment.

"Except you have an aunt who's going out with my dad."

"You think that's the connection? You think they're smart enough to figure all that out?"

"Who knows? Maybe not. Maybe it *is* just a coincidence. Maybe there are lots of other Jewish families getting these calls."

"Yeah, and the hate mail went in everyone's locker, not just mine. Or maybe Roger noticed me because I noticed him. He checked me out, found out I'm Jewish—it could've started that way." I pause. "Of course Aunt Janeen believes that everything happens for a reason, that there are no accidents."

Jon smiles. "Do you?"

I think for a moment. "Science is full of accidents.

Most of the big discoveries have been made by accident. Also, a lot of the way subatomic particles work seems to be random."

Jon laughs. "Well, maybe they're all *meant* to be random, and the accidents were *meant* to happen!"

"Yeah," I grin, "that must be it!" I look at my watch. "Should we go retrieve our tape?"

Getting the tape goes smoothly and we drive back to my place to listen to it. We sit in the basement and play it. At first there's nothing. The sound of the dog, the owner, Klaus, calling to it, muttering as he looks out the windows. More silence. Then the sound of machinery running. Very loud.

"I wonder what that is?" Jon says.

I play it again. It has a repetitious sound, almost like the photocopier in the office. Suddenly I know. It's a printer. "I'll bet they're printing that stuff right there!" I exclaim. This sound goes on for a good thirty minutes and finally shuts off. And then we hear voices! Muffled, but loud enough to make out what they're saying.

"This looks good. 'We let in the Jews, they took over our banks, our schools, our media. Now the government wants to let in anyone. But it's up to us to stop them! Rise up, brothers! Help us create a

Christian world, pure, clean, and holy. Rise up and strike down the devils!' Great stuff."

I hear the voice again. "Couldn't we mail them, too?"

"No," another voice says. "We do it as planned. We use these to target certain people, try to get them to our next meeting. It's not for general release."

Then there's static and we can't hear anything. Then: ". . . the plan going?" "Good." "Everything on schedule?" "If this doesn't scare them off nothing will." "It will. Dead people always scare the living." "It'll scare that vermin."

Then the sound of footsteps. Then nothing.

Jon and I stare at each other.

"We should play this for your dad," I say.

"Can I take it home with me?"

"You'd better. Mom and Dad will never let me out again tonight. But call me as soon as he's heard it. He can take it to the police for us. They'll *have* to do something now."

Jon looks really upset.

"Don't worry," I say, "the police will get them before they—"

"Before they manage to blow up Dad, or me, or my brothers?" he says bitterly.

"I hope so. Or," I mutter, "someone from *my* family. We don't know who they're after, do we?"

"They're after *us*," he says. "I think the car bomb proved that. I don't understand why that isn't enough to go on! Why don't the police just arrest the guy?"

"I don't understand it either," I say. "Anyway, this must be the proof they need."

Jon takes my hand. "You've been great," he says. "I never would have thought of doing anything like this. Maybe in your last life you fought in the resistance against the Nazis! You almost seem like you've done this before."

Although I want to laugh when he says it, something inside me wonders whether he's right. It *does* feel like I've done this before—after all, creeping about spying on people isn't exactly a normal activity for a fifteen-year-old.

"Maybe our friend Klaus has already murdered me," I say, making a lame joke.

"In the war, you mean?" he says, taking me perfectly seriously. "And now you've returned in this body to help put him away. It's possible."

"It *is*?" This is Jon's territory, I guess, this reincarnation stuff.

"It is," says Jon, looking very thoughtful.

"Jade!" calls Mom. "It's bedtime."

"You'd better go," I say.

"Right," he agrees. "I'll call you later. If Dad's not home or something, it may have to wait till morning. I don't want to wake up your parents and get them any madder at me than they already are."

"They aren't mad at you," I say.

"They probably haven't *told* you they are," he says, "but who do you think they blame for all this going out in the middle of the week?"

"Me?"

"No, not their own daughter. They're probably beginning to think I'm a bad influence on you." He's still holding my hand, which is practically burning in his. And now he looks me in the eye. And his eyes are *so* gorgeous, I could just melt. And he leans over, slowly, so slowly it's like it's taking a million years, and he kisses me really softly on the lips. It's the most perfect kiss I've ever had in my entire life. I can see why heroines tended to faint in the old days. I feel quite dizzy.

He drops my hand and clutching the tape in the other moves up the stairs. I have to catch my breath and force myself off the spot I'm rooted to.

When he gets to the door, Dad is there. He wishes him good night and he's gone.

"Up to bed, Jade," says Dad.

I float up to bed and it's not until much later that I even remember the tape, Klaus, and the weird conversation about reincarnation. I stay up for ages waiting for the phone to ring, just wanting to hear the sound of Jon's voice again, but the phone won't ring, and eventually I drift off to sleep. And I dream. The same dream. The car blows up. And I *know* it's not about what's already happened. But if that's all I know—what good is it?

FIFTEEN

JON CALLS IN THE MORNING BEFORE SCHOOL. He tells me he played the tape for his dad late last night after his dad had come home from a meeting.

"And?" I say.

"And he says the police can't use it."

"What?"

"It's an illegal tap. You can't eavesdrop on someone without a warrant. And they can't even use this to *get* a warrant."

"You're kidding, right?"

"Wrong. I'm sorry, Jade. I should have thought of that myself."

"So these guys can go around making this stuff and *nothing* will happen?"

"Actually, Dad is going to take the tape with him to the police department. Once they hear it they may be able to figure out a way to get a warrant. They may even be able to investigate on a zoning law—like, is he allowed to have a printer operating in that neighbourhood. Dad's going to try to figure *something* out. Or help the police do it."

I sigh. "That's good. But I wonder what it is they're planning."

"So do I. Wish I had a crystal ball. Jade? Jade?"

I've practically stopped breathing. I *do* have a crystal ball, of course—inside me. But how do I get it to work? Someone is in danger, and I have to find out who and try to stop it.

"I have to go," I say, "talk to you later."

"Yeah." Pause. "It was a strange night last night," he says, "but I had fun."

"Me too," I say, hoping I'm not putting all the feeling in my voice that's really there. "See you."

"See you."

I put down the receiver but pick it up again almost immediately and call Baba.

"Baba, I have to talk to you about, well, about these powers you think I have."

"Why, sweetheart?"

"I'm having this dream, and I'm sure it's some kind of warning, but I can't figure out what kind."

"I'll pick you up right after school," Baba says. "I know exactly where we need to go. Lucky I'm so far ahead with my baking."

Tomorrow is Yom Kippur, and the next day we all go to Baba's to break the fast. She cooks for weeks ahead of time.

At school I find my mind wandering equally among Jon's kiss, the horrible things we heard on the tape, and my dream. One second I'm dreaming of more kisses, the next I'm panic-stricken over what these maniacs might do. How do people get filled with so much hate? I think Mr. Crossley is right. Fear. They are terrified. I remember last year we had an author visiting the school, and this author said that evil is really the need to control other people. That stuck with me because I thought about things—from kids making each other's lives miserable to Hitler—and what was the one thing they had in common? Control. And maybe it's true that the need to control comes from fear. I'm only fifteen. I wish I didn't have to worry or even think about stuff like this. But I do. I can't run away from it any more, I know that.

After school Baba picks me up.

"I'm taking you to a psychic I've been going to for years," she says.

"*You* go to psychics?" I exclaim.

"She went to school with me," Baba explains. "And she really had the gift. Still does. I think she can help you because she's been through everything."

"Baba," I say, "do you believe everything is fated?"

Baba glances at me for a moment, making me sorry I asked. Baba's one big failing is that she is an *awful* driver. I can't wait until I'm sixteen and *I* can drive when we go out together. As she weaves in between two lanes—her favourite way to drive is right down the dividing line—she considers my question.

"There's a Jewish expression," she answers, finally. "*B'shert*. It means that things are meant to be. I *do* believe that. I believe God has a plan for all of us."

"So where's our free will?" I ask.

"Our challenge is to figure out what God's plan is," she replies. "And, of course, we can choose to follow it or not. And even if we aren't thinking about the big picture, we have choices all the time."

"But Baba, how can you believe in God after the Holocaust?" I ask.

"Jade," she sighs, "that is the biggest question of our day for Jews. But I say that God didn't make the Holocaust. Hitler and those that collaborated with him made it happen. *They* made those choices."

"Do you see God as, like, a person?"

"No, no!" Baba laughs. "God is the *Ein Sof*, the unknowable, not a man sitting on a cloud. And somehow, darling, you are able to tap into that."

"Maybe," I reply. "But Dr. Manuel thinks I could be tapping into the way time is—I think Einstein talked about that a lot."

"And," Baba nods, "Einstein believed in God. He thought the universe was too miraculous not to."

A car behind us honks. Another swerves to avoid us. I'll bet this unknowable one gets a lot of prayers when Baba is on the road!

SIXTEEN

Baba's friend, Frieda Konantz, is short and plump with bleach-blond hair all pouffed up and jewellery everywhere—big rings on all her fingers, long gold chains, dangling gold earrings. She lives in an apartment block on Wellington Crescent, only a few minutes from my school. Her living-room window looks out over the Assiniboine River. I guess either she or her husband must have also had a "normal" kind of business or she wouldn't live in such a nice place. The aura around her is a bright yellowish white, and she settles me on a deep sofa covered in red flowers with a white background. She takes my hand and looks in my eyes.

"Jade. Beautiful name."

I smile. "It's the only different thing Mom and Dad have ever done—name me Jade, I mean."

"Which shows that they do have an unconventional streak," Mrs. Konantz says. "It's there, just small. Your Baba tells me that you're having trouble dealing with your powers."

I nod.

"Wait!" She holds up her hand. "Oy! Naomi!" She stares at my Baba.

Baba's eyes open wide. "What! What is it?"

"I hate to tell you, but not all your grandchildren will marry Jewish children," she says.

"Is that all?" Baba says. "You scared me half to death. I could have told you that!"

"Fine," says Frieda, her bracelets clanking as she lowers her arms. She stares at me and nods.

"I had some trouble dealing with my powers when I was young," she remarks. "But I always had powers. I thought everyone did. When I discovered they *didn't*, that was the big shock."

"Kind of the opposite of me," I say.

"True. But I still had to deal with people who were afraid of me, and people who thought I was crazy."

"But you never thought you were crazy?"

She laughs. She has a funny hiccuppy kind of laugh. "I thought *I* was the normal one until I was around ten years old. Then when I found out not everyone could see what I could see, I felt a bit sorry for them. Of course, now I realize that it's both a curse and a blessing."

"Like how?" I ask.

"How!" she repeats. "Try going shopping when every person you pass has a story to tell, if they only knew it! Try going to a party and not letting on you know who's being unfaithful to who, that the hostess used a cheap caterer and the cheese is a little off, the daughter has just run off to join a cult . . . Well, you get the idea!"

Great, I think to myself, this is making me feel *lots* better.

"I feel like such a freak, though," I complain.

"I know, dear," she says, patting my hand. "But that's because people, in general, have been taught to believe only what they can see. Your Baba tells me you're a scientist."

"Yeah, kind of."

"Can you see, what are those things, sounds like a duck?"

I grin. "A quark?"

"Yes! That's it! My, you're clever."

"You can't see them, but you can surmise them from mathematical formulas," I explain.

"And if you predict something and it comes true, that's pretty real, isn't it?"

I shrug.

"I was watching TV the other night," she continues, "and I saw a piece on a young man who can echo-locate—you know, that's what bats and whales do, that's how they 'see.' Well, this young man is blind but he taught himself how to 'see' by using the same kind of clicking noises bats and whales use. He makes this clicking noise with his tongue, it echoes off his surroundings, and by listening he can judge exactly where everything is. They showed pictures of him. He was riding a bike! He walked with no cane or help at all. It was amazing. And he's teaching it to others." She pauses. "So you see we only use a very small portion of our brain. I think you and I, Jade, have tapped into something that most people have—they just don't use it. And you know, different psychics often have different gifts. One can divine water, another can heal, another can fix anything. Perhaps they are just tapping into different portions of their brain." And she taps her head, bracelets clanking, to illustrate her point.

"So it's not like this big religious thing or anything," I say.

She smiles. "I didn't say that. Actually, I'm not sure.

'Religious' is a funny word. I just think the unseen world is as real as the one we think we see. I believe in an afterlife, of course, because I can talk to the spirits at times. They are as real as we are. And Jade, I can see three spirit guides hovering around you."

"You can?"

"Oh, yes. We all have some, you know. And if you listen, you can hear it when they speak. Or they will help you hear your own inner voice."

"Who are they?" I ask, really curious.

"I don't know," she answers. "I could probably find out but that's not what we're here for today. You have a big worry."

"I keep having this dream and it scares me. I need to know what to do."

"Describe it to me," she says.

As I talk she begins to lay out cards. "These are Tarot cards," she says when I finish telling her the dream. "Really, they simply help me focus." She closes her eyes for just a moment. "You have a friend, a boy, dark skin, good looking, very nice, he will be very important to you."

I glance at Baba.

She shakes her head like, no, I didn't tell her about Jon.

"I can see you're having trouble at school, but that will change slowly. Soon everyone will be coming to you, begging you to read their cards and tell their future. Tell them that you can't read people so young, everything changes too fast."

"But I can."

She raises her eyebrows.

"You'll have to find your own way to control it. Warning people if you think it'll help, otherwise staying quiet."

I know I shouldn't interrupt but I have to. "But that's the trouble," I exclaim. "How on earth am I supposed to know when to tell something and when not to? I mean, what if I tell something, just a little thing, like you really have to study for this test or you'll fail, and they *do* study and don't fail and go on to, like, university say, and then into politics, and they become the person who takes over the world. And if they'd failed they would've become a business person or a plumber and never would have hurt anyone!"

Mrs. Konantz and Baba stare at each other.

"She's a tough one, I told you," Baba says.

Mrs. Konantz nods. She thinks for a minute. "Well, Jade, either you were *meant* to intervene or you'll just have to take a chance, won't you? Just because you can see the future doesn't necessarily mean it's fixed. Maybe all you're seeing is the most likely outcome."

"I read in a book once that the future is like a fan—and the stands of the fan are all the various futures, depending on what choices we make."

Mrs. Konantz nods. "Just so. Now let's have a look at your dream." She finishes laying out the cards. She looks up at me.

"Can you remember anything else about it?"

"No," I say. "I'm sure that's all, just this guy, the grey car, Marty, an explosion, lots of bodies."

"I see it, Jade. Damages, many people hurt, you get hurt too but I see people close to you . . ." She stops. She turns a little pale. I notice that her aura darkens.

"You don't think I can do anything!" I accuse her. "You think something terrible is going to happen and I can't stop it. Can't you see what it is?"

She shakes her head and takes my hand. "But it's not just a few people. It's lots of people. And you *can* do something. If you keep your head and don't assume—don't assume that what you see is real, look beneath the surface. Remember that."

She drops my hand. Baba gets up. "You're tired," Baba says.

"I'm afraid so, dear," Mrs. Konantz says. "It takes it out of me a bit now," she concedes. She pats my hand. "You take care, dear. Take care."

"I will," I say, my voice shaky. I mean, it sounds like it's going to be up to me to stop this catastrophe, but I'm still no closer to finding out what it is or how to stop it. And she didn't say it but I could tell—she saw my death too, along with all the others.

SEVENTEEN

I WALK INTO THE HOUSE AND MOM IS FRANTIC. "Where have you been?" she demands. "We have to eat early, Jade, you know that. The service starts in an hour."

We have a service tonight and tomorrow at the synagogue, and, of course, everyone wants to eat because as of sundown we fast until sundown tomorrow.

"Oh, and Jon called. Said it was important."

I turn to call him back.

"*After* dinner," Mom says. "We're eating *now*."

Well, that's a tone of voice I don't hear too often, so I wash my hands and meekly sit down with Marty and Dad, who are looking at me like, good choice, Jade.

No one says I can't eat fast, though. And I do. Despite the fact that Mom is grilling me about where Baba and I went and what happened. At first I don't want to tell them—I know how Mom will react. But they keep at me until I do. So I tell them that we went over to Mrs. Konantz's so she could help me because she's been a psychic all her life.

"You know," says Mom, "she may just be able to pick up cues and body language that other people can't see. I think that accounts for a lot of this."

Exactly how I knew she'd react. And she wonders why I no longer want to talk to her about all this.

"I suppose that would explain how she described Jon to a T," I mumble, mouth full of salad.

"Well, Baba could have mentioned him."

"She didn't! Unless you think your own mother is trying to scam you—and me."

"No, of course I don't think that," Mom says.

"Well?"

Mom shakes her head. "I don't know."

"You and I may have to reexamine our way of looking at the world," Dad says, to Mom. "But isn't that what children are best at?"

"Making us old guys see things differently?" Mom asks.

Dad nods.

Mom smiles ruefully. "I guess so. All right, Jade, go and call Jon. But no more than five minutes on the phone. You still have to get changed."

I grab the half of the roast potato still left on my plate and take it with me to chew as I talk, then run up to my room.

Jon answers on the first ring. "Jade! Great news."

"What?"

"The police were so disgusted by that tape that they managed to get a warrant based on the zoning restriction in that area. They can't use the tape at all, but if they find any evidence they should be able to start rounding up the group."

"When are they going in?" I ask.

"First thing tomorrow morning."

"Tomorrow," I sigh. "But what about . . . ?"

I stop myself. I almost said, "What about my dream?" And then I'd end up telling him everything, and that's no good.

"What about what?"

"Nothing. Couldn't they go sooner?"

"I don't think so. They're getting the warrant now, I think, and arranging a whole team for the morning." He pauses. "You did it, Jade! If these are the guys going after us, maybe the police will find enough evidence to at least hurry the extradition of Schmidt, or maybe even put him away here."

"Yeah," I say.

"You don't sound happy."

"No, I am, really. It's just—well, how many are there? How do we know they'll catch them all? And what else are they planning?"

"You're right, I guess," Jon sighs. "It may take a while to catch them all. But if their leader is taken away that has to help."

"Sure it will," I say, not wanting to worry him any more. But somehow this news isn't making me feel better. It's great, of course, but I don't think it's going to stop this trouble I keep dreaming about. In fact, I *know*, somehow, that it isn't.

"Listen, Jon, it's Yom Kippur tonight so I have to run."

"Will you be at synagogue all day tomorrow?" he asks.

"No. We go in the morning, then again in the late afternoon," I say.

"So I'll call you after lunch," Jon says, "and let you know what happened."

"Great," I say. "Talk to you then."

"Happy New Year," he says.

"Thanks." He's so sweet. He even remembers what the holiday is and everything.

"Repent all your sins!" he adds.

"Yeah," I laugh, "I will."

I get changed quickly and brush my hair, which by now seems to be a mass of tangles. I don't wear make-up so I don't have to worry about that. I'm actually ready before Mom.

Tonight both Marty and I will go to the service, but tomorrow morning he'll be in a special youth service downstairs and I'll be doing my volunteer work with the little kids. I've been a youth leader at the synagogue ever since my Bat Mitzvah. It has great advantages. First of all you don't have to sit through the boring service, and second of all you don't have to sit through the boring service! I look after the children ages six through nine. They're really cute. Marcie, the other youth leader I'm paired with, and I read them stories, play games with them, and of course, most importantly, give them their snacks. This can be difficult when you're fasting, and I must admit that two years ago I scarfed down five cookies when no one was looking, but last year I had more self-control.

The closer we get to synagogue the queasier I start to feel. Almost sick to my stomach. I put it down to eating dinner too fast and try to ignore it.

I actually like the evening Yom Kippur service, called Kol Nidre. Tonight, our new cantor, a woman, sings the service and it is so beautiful that almost everyone is crying at one point or another—even me. The melodies are so haunting and it's all so sad in a way, thinking about all the things you've done wrong over the last year. You are supposed to use the ten days in between Rosh Hashanah and Yom Kippur to fix any feuds you're having with people so you can start everything in the New Year fresh, and in that ten days God decides what your next year will be like and writes it in a book on Yom Kippur. So according to that, everything is decided as of tomorrow. Why bother making any choices, I wonder. Maybe you have to make good choices so *next* year God will give you a good year. But, you see, this is what bugs me. It makes God seem like some guy sitting up there, judging. I can't relate to that. No, I like Aunt Janeen's ideas better. And Baba's. I guess that's one good thing about being Jewish, there are a million ways to do it.

When the rabbi gives his sermon it's about the hate mail we received at school. He talks about fear and hatred and how we Jews are so often the brunt of all of that. And he encourages us to do something, get involved. Well, at least I can say I've done that.

When we get home, I'm exhausted and go straight to bed. My stomach feels better once I'm home but I feel too tired to stay awake. Sometime during the night I dream, and I wake up again, in a sweat. It's the same dream. Except this time I see the car, then I'm inside somewhere, and I look around because I *have* to find out where I am. I'm in synagogue. And then the car explodes.

EIGHTEEN

I RUN INTO MY PARENTS' ROOM AND WAKE THEM UP.

"My dream! I had it again. It's the synagogue. They're going to car bomb the synagogue. When lots of people are there. Maybe today!"

Dad is patting my back. Mom is too groggy to speak at first.

"What time is it?" Dad asks.

I look at their clock. "Three o'clock."

"Jade," Dad says, "it's just a dream."

"An anxiety dream," Mom says. "You were in synagogue today, and your mind just stuck that into the dream about the car."

"On the other hand," Dad says, "someone *did* blow up Sahjit's car. And they haven't caught who did it, or who's distributing this hate mail."

"Yes, but why assume whoever attacked Sahjit is connected to the hate mail in any way?" Mom says.

"But they are!" I exclaim. "See, Jon and I kind of followed that creep Roger and he's involved with this Nazi Sahjit is trying to get out of the country, and I made a microphone and we taped them talking, and they *are* planning something. The police are on to them now but it may be too late!"

"Jade!" Mom is now wide awake. "I can't *believe* you didn't tell us any of this before."

"I knew you'd worry," I mumble. "And you couldn't have done anything."

"We could've stopped you from putting yourself in danger like that!" Mom says.

"Exactly!" I reply. "That's why I didn't tell you!"

"I think you were very resourceful," Dad says. "I'm proud of you."

"David!"

"Well, she was. There's the rabbi talking to us about *doing* something, yet you'd rather she did nothing? Besides, it sounds like she *was* careful."

Mom shakes her head. "Honestly, this entire family has lost all their sense."

"And you know something else?" Dad says, "I think Jade is right. I'm going to call Len Berman. As president of the synagogue he's better able to talk to the police. I think all cars should be searched for bombs. Better safe than sorry. After all, what better target for a bunch of anti-Semites than a synagogue on Yom Kippur. I won't mention Jade's dreams, I'll just remind him about the hate mail and tell him about the threats—that should be enough."

Mom is quiet for a moment. "I think you're right," she says. "We'd better do something. Don't worry, honey," she says to me, "Dad and I will call Len, first thing in the morning. You go back to sleep."

"Call him now," I say.

"I'll call at six o'clock," Dad says. "That should give everyone enough time."

"No, Dad, it won't," I say. "What if the police don't believe him at first? The service starts at eight tomorrow."

"She's right," Mom agrees. "If we're going to call we may as well do it now."

Dad turns on the light. He goes downstairs to find Mr. Berman's phone number. Mom walks me back to my room.

"We'll take care of it, sweetheart," she says. "You go back to bed."

"I'll never sleep."

"Then just lie and rest and listen to music," Mom says.

I climb back into bed and put on some real cheesy eighties stuff I like to listen to when I'm stressed. And somehow I fall asleep.

~

When I wake up it's seven o'clock and Mom is shaking me.

"Time to get up, Jade. Go take your shower."

I look at the clock.

"Mom! I'm late. The little kids start to get there right at eight and I have to be there."

"Jade, maybe you should stay home this morning. Maybe we all should."

"No!" I scream, startling her with my reaction. "I *have* to be there."

"Why?"

"I don't know. I just do. But you can stay home . . ."

"No, Dad is determined to go. He's talked to the president and the police have agreed to bring their dogs, the ones that sniff out explosives. Everyone will be checked driving into the parking lot and cars will be checked by the dogs. Of course Len is having a fit about the traffic jam this is all going to cause, but Dad reminded him of the alternative. The police are being terrific. I'm sure they'll have it all under control."

I hurry with my shower, and since I can't eat I'm ready in ten minutes. I find Marty in the kitchen eating a huge breakfast. His Bar Mitzvah isn't until next year, when he's thirteen, so he doesn't have to fast until then. My stomach is feeling queasy again, though, so I'm not even tempted. Both Mom and Dad look pretty bad, like they've been up all night—which they have.

It's a short drive to the synagogue on Wellington Crescent. There is a driveway which leads to a parking lot at the back of the synagogue. There is also a large parking lot on the side. Behind the back lot is the river bank and the Assiniboine River. Traffic is backed up already as each car is stopped, checked by two policemen and a sniffing dog. By the time we get parked it is after eight and I'm late for my kids.

On the way to the front doors everyone stops everyone else and asks if there's been a bomb threat, what has happened. Mr. Berman is standing by the front door and is explaining as people hurry in that there's been no threat, to relax, that these are just precautions. He tells Dad that the synagogue itself was checked out by the dogs and they found nothing.

Dad pats my shoulder. "Okay, Jade? Is that better?"

I try to smile and nod. But inside I feel sick. Inside, something is telling me that it isn't better. That somehow it's still going to happen. Then my "reasonable" side takes over. After all, it's just a dream. Probably no more than that. And with all these precautions what could possibly happen?

I take a deep breath, say goodbye to Mom and Dad, then turn to go downstairs with Marty. Suddenly I turn back and give them each a hug. Before the surprised looks on their faces are gone I'm pushing Marty ahead of me down the stairs. Mom and Dad will go into the sanctuary, Marty goes into the large room where the older kids are having their service, and I head for my little classroom down the hall, past the coat room. A number of little ones are already there, and so is Marcie.

"Hi," she says brightly. Marcie is a little annoying. As usual she's dressed in the latest fashion, her hair recently dyed and so many holes in her ears I've given up counting. That's fine, but I've often worried that the holes in her ears are somehow leaking grey matter.

"Really cool out there, huh?"

And I know she's not referring to the weather.

"I wouldn't exactly call it cool, Marcie."

"I would!" she declares. "It's always so boring around here. It sure woke me up when I realized a dog was sniffing our car for bombs."

I shake my head. I mean, what can you say?

More children start to arrive, their parents frantically trying to get up to the service. Many of them have duties to perform or special readings to give and they're afraid they're late.

At about nine Mike comes in with our box of apple juices and the cookies. I unpack the juice boxes and get them ready, even though we won't give them out for another hour. I can't seem to get focused on the games. I must admit, though, Marcie is great with the kids. She has endless energy, and the little ones just love her.

My stomach starts to feel worse and worse and my head starts to pound. I feel horrible. Dread is settling over me, draping me like a heavy blanket. I excuse myself, go to the bathroom, splash cold water on my face. It doesn't help. I return to the room just as a dark-haired man wearing a *kipah* is leaving. I go over to the window and look out over the parking lot.

Marty pokes his head in. "Hey," he says, "need any help? Our service is super boring."

I'm about to say no but Marcie can't say no to anyone! "Sure. Come on in. You can help the kids with the colouring."

I glance out the window again. In the first row of cars by the synagogue is a grey car. My heart stops. There must be lots of grey cars in the lot, I tell myself. So what? But Marty comes over to me, and says, "Jade, are there any extra crayons around?"

Marty is here. The car. I thought I'd be outside with the car but I see it, I hear him.

"Oh," Marcie calls to Marty, "that man brought in a box of supplies just a few minutes ago."

She points to a square box on a table by the door taped up tightly.

Everything is not as it seems. Not as it looks. See beneath the surface. I hear Mrs. Konantz's voice. Listen to yourself.

Marty starts to walk over to the package. He picks it up, turns it over. "Boy, is this taped up." He puts it back on the table. He goes over to one of the children. "May I borrow your scissors, please?"

I walk over to the box. I stare at it. Marty is beside me. "Jade, can you move?"

I pick up the box. We didn't ask for supplies. They

never give us extra supplies. And I've never seen that man before.

The box in my hands, I turn and run out of the room. I head for the back door. I scream at the usher standing by the door, "Open the door, open it!" He does. I race through the lot and I pass the grey car and I know I only have seconds. I run a few more steps until I'm at the riverbank and then I heave the box with all my might.

There is a huge sound, like a mountain exploding, and then something hits me and I'm knocked off my feet into the grass. My head is swimming, everything has gone fuzzy and wavy like heat lines on the highway. I can hear someone calling me from far away and people are screaming and I hear footsteps and sirens and then I close my eyes and for a while there is a blissful silence.

NINETEEN

I OPEN MY EYES TO SEE AN AMBULANCE WORKER doing something to my forehead. I'm lying flat on the ground, and all the sounds are still there, sirens, noise, although the screams seem to have died down. Mom, Dad, and Marty are all hovering around me. Mom's face is white as a sheet. Dad is holding my hand.

"What happened?" I croak.

"You threw a bomb into the river," Marty grins. "No one's gonna call *you* names any more. It was *so* cool. Just like in the movies."

"The blast knocked you over and you've probably got a very slight concussion," the medic says. "I think we should take her in just to be on the safe side," he says to my parents.

"Can I ride in the ambulance with you?" Marty asks the driver.

The medic looks at him. "If it's okay with your sister."

I try to nod but my head hurts when I move it.

"We'll follow behind you," Mom says, and she and Dad walk beside the stretcher as they carry me to the ambulance. Dad is still holding my hand.

"How could you know?" he says to me.

"I just *knew*," I whisper.

He really stares at me then, as if his whole world might just be about to turn upside down.

"Man oh man," says Marty, "when are you gonna get it through your head, Dad, Jade can *see* stuff."

"I think I just got it," Dad says.

"The bomb squad was right outside," Mom says, no longer able to contain herself, "you couldn't have called them? You had to run outside with a bomb in your hands?" She's shaking from head to foot.

Dad gently lets go of my hand and puts his arms around Mom.

"She's fine. We're all fine."

Mom starts to cry.

They load me into the ambulance, Marty right beside me. I'm glad he's along. I guess little brothers aren't quite as bad as mosquitoes.

I must have drifted off again because I do not remember anything else until I wake up in the hospital bed. Aunt Janeen is there, and Baba and Mom, Dad, and Marty. Aunt Janeen goes to an alternative service in the North End so it must be well into the afternoon if she's here, and Baba was probably home cooking when Mom or Dad called.

I can see colours all around them and I can tell they're worried about me, all except Baba. She gives me a little wink, like she knew all along I'd pull it off. I giggle to myself. Probably Zaida told her.

TWENTY

JON AND I ARE WALKING IN THE ENGLISH GARDENS in Assiniboine Park. The sky is a pure prairie blue, the leaves are just starting to change, and there are still lots of flowers in full bloom. We saunter along. I've been talking steadily since we got here, telling Jon everything. Now there is silence. I had to tell him. Aunt Janeen immediately blabbed to Sahjit, and Jon was going to find out. I figured it was better if he heard it all from me.

The same morning that they tried to blow up the synagogue a team got into Schmidt's house with a search warrant. They found the printer all ready to run off another batch of hate mail. They've arrested him and Roger and about ten others. It is the biggest conspiracy this city has ever had to deal with. They've kept my part in it from the papers, though, just in case there are any others from the group who weren't caught. As for how the bomb got past the dogs—apparently one of them had placed it in the synagogue fridge the night before, behind some egg salad which had been prepared for breaking the fast. The dogs must have been confused by too many smells. But what really, really upsets me is the thought that it wasn't enough for them to leave the bomb in the fridge so it would go off there. After all, with an empty kitchen maybe no one would die. They brought it to a room full of children. Children! Every time I think about it I feel sick.

Jon takes my hand and we sit down on a bench. "Can you tell what I'm thinking now?"

"No!" I exclaim. I pause. "Not really."

"Come on, Jade," he says, "be honest."

"Well, I mean, once people get to know each other they can often tell what the other person is thinking, right? Like they can read each other's minds. This isn't that different. I'll bet you can tell what I'm thinking. Try."

Jon looks at me for a moment. Oh, those eyes!

"You're probably a little worried about how I'm going to react to this," he says.

Whew. Not even close. All I can think of are those big brown eyes. Well, not true. Of course I'm worried. I'm terrified.

“There!” I declare. “See? It’s just I can do it with people I hardly know.”

“But Jade, you see into the future, too.” He grins. “So, you should know how I’ll react.”

I grin back. “You’re right. But it doesn’t seem to work that way. Although, I think if I try to develop these skills, maybe I’ll be able to have more control.”

“Now I see why you’re so interested in God and all that,” Jon says. “I would be too, in your shoes.”

“Yeah, like what does it all mean?”

“Maybe you don’t have to figure out what it all means right away, Jade,” he says. “Maybe as you grow older you’ll just start to *know* what it all means.”

Man, I like this guy.

“Do you mind?” I ask.

“Well, I’d be lying to you if I didn’t admit that it’s kind of weird. I mean, we all like our privacy.”

“I’d never eavesdrop on purpose,” I assure him. “But,” I have to admit, “sometimes I can’t help it.”

He takes my hand again and we get up to continue our walk.

“I’ll let you know,” he says, “if it gets too weird.” Then he bends over and kisses me.

And I don’t need any special powers to know what both of us are feeling.

EPILOGUE

I've decided to write all this down, even though writing is hard for me, because if this thing runs in families, I'd like my granddaughter (how do I know it'll be her? I just do!) to have an idea of what I went through. Maybe it'll help her. I hope so.

Baba gave me some passages to read from a very famous Jewish philosopher, Moses Maimonides, because I was bugging her again about free will and the future.

"Every man is granted free will. If he desires to incline towards the good way and be righteous, he has the power to do so; and if he desires to incline towards the unrighteous way, and be a wicked man, he also has the power to do so."

Baba says we can choose the path that God means us to take, and Aunt Janeen says that our spirit has already chosen our path before we are born, and Sahjit says we follow the path of our karma, and Mom and Dad are just pretty darned confused right now.

And me? I'm following Jon's advice. I'm just trying to do the right thing day by day and one day, I hope, eventually, it'll all make sense to me. And if that's too much to ask—well then, I guess I'll have to learn to live with it.